To Dearest John,
Much Love, Christmas 19~.
Love Lyn. xxxx

CW00405039

Malayan Patrol

Malayan Patrol

by

E. T. Boddye

The Pentland Press Limited
Edinburgh · Cambridge · Durham

First published in 1993 by
The Pentland Press Ltd.
1 Hutton Close
South Church
Bishop Auckland
Durham

ISBN 1 85821 038 0

Typeset by Elite Typesetting Techniques, Southampton.
Printed and bound by Antony Rowe Ltd., Chippenham.

Contents

Foreword

The most successful counter-insurgency operation conducted by Britain since World War II, with the help of her Commonwealth allies, was in Malaya. From 1948, Communist terrorists, or bandits as they were called in the earlier years, tried to inflict their creed on the population. By murder, propaganda and hoped-for civil unrest they planned to force the British troops and administration prematurely out of Malaya.

During the Japanese occupation, the Communist guerillas with assistance in training and a supply of arms from the British, resisted the invaders. Little over two years after Japan surrendered the Communist Party, realising they were failing to gain control of the country by organising strikes and political dissension, returned to the jungle to begin an armed offensive. They armed themselves with the weapons which, with foresight, they had stockpiled during the occupation. By terror and murder they set about creating 'liberated areas'.

The Malays, with few exceptions, together with the majority of Chinese and Indians, had little sympathy for the bandits. There inevitably was a hard core of supporters who supplied them with food and information. Those who didn't help, particularly those suspected of supplying information to the Security Forces, ran the ever-present risk of being killed. Planters, Police and the Army were ambushed; police stations and planters' bungalows were attacked. This was in the early days before the bandits started to lose the initiative.

It has been said that, in those early days, some senior statesmen and soldiers wondered whether the bandits could ever be completely defeated. This was not a thought that crossed the minds of 8 Platoon, C Company of the 1st Battalion, The Yorkshire Fusiliers, on the rare occasions they discussed such weighty matters over a bottle of cold beer in the canteen.

vii

The problem, as they saw it, was to find the bandits in the first place and then make them stand up and fight.

That the Emergency, as it was known, was brought to a successful conclusion was due to the combined efforts of the Army, RAF, Police and Administrators. The British Army's contribution was many battalions which included in their ranks many hundreds of National Servicemen. These were men, conscripted for two years who, after basic training in the U.K., were sent halfway round the world into the Malayan jungle; an environment far removed from the towns and villages from which they came. These conscripts, serving as private soldiers, junior non-commissioned officers and platoon commanders, followed the Regimental traditions of the battalions to which they were posted. This is an account of the experiences of a National Service Officer and his Platoon. It describes their successes and disappointments, long periods of inaction and occasional violent incidents. Names of units and individuals have been changed but the events described are based on what actually happened in the jungle of Malaya.

Introduction

'I suppose it was.' Byrne put down Colonel Spencer Chapman's *The Jungle is Neutral*. The book described Colonel Chapman's experiences with Force 136 in the Malayan jungle after the fall of Singapore. His was a torrid story of a long guerilla war alongside the Chinese guerillas against the Japanese. Andrew Byrne thought back over forty years to his own little war. Chinese, Indians, Malays or British – all got soaked, bitten by mosquitoes and if very unlucky, had the painful experience of being bitten by the Red Tree-Ant, when the only remedy was to strip the clothing off the affected parts of the body to remove the fiercely biting insects; a ritual performed with all possible speed. Bandits or soldiers no doubt stood on a high place at one time and were entranced by the rich green jungle-covered hills, the blue sky above and perhaps, in the foothills, wisps of early-morning mists still lingering. He remembered an off-duty visit to the beaches of Malacca. One day he would go back. Many times he had told his wife that the sand was golden, the palm trees were green and the sea bright blue and warm. She would love Malaysia in peace-time. She would delight in the colourful sarongs, the endless variety of shops, the clinks of the tiles from the games of mah-jong being played in the coffee houses. He would hire a car, stop on the way north from Singapore, walk a little way into the jungle and breathe again that never to be forgotten warm fetid air.

There would be no-one for him to visit. The older planters he had known would have died long ago, the younger retired far from the plantations he had once patrolled. Some he knew had died violent deaths; hospitable, cheerful men, victims of ambushes they had seen too late or not at all. Not long before he had left C Company for Singapore to fly home, he had been offered a job as Assistant Manager on one of the biggest estates in Negri Sembilan. He had been momentarily tempted by the size of the salary on offer compared with his Second Lieutenant's pay. However, even if family, girlfriend and university hadn't beckoned him home, he knew he could not easily have faced the prospect of doing the daily rounds of a plantation in the company of two special constables instead of in the security of his beloved 8 Platoon.

Though a long time ago, he still remembered much. Some names had long since been forgotten but he would never forget the cheerfulness and enthusiasm of his Platoon. Eighteen year-old National Servicemen sent into the jungle because that was where their County Regiment happened to be. They had done well. One-time Second Lieutenant Byrne recalled when it all began.

THE MALAYAN PENINSULA

xi

Chapter 1

The Recruit

October 1950 was a fine month. Not that Fusilier Byrne had much time to appreciate the weather after reporting to the Army Basic Training Unit on the instructions of the War Office. Realising the inevitability of National Service, Byrne had taken two precautions to prepare for the day he walked through the barrack gates. Firstly, two years before, he had joined the Army Cadet Force. Though three years older than the other new Cadets and on average, a foot taller, he had endured this initially minor embarrassment without too much difficulty when, on his first parade, he was put in the Recruits Cadre. Since that date, once a week he had walked down to the old Drill Hall in the evening to be instructed in, what he eventually discovered to be, pre-World War II foot drill, by a venerable Sergeant Major. More intellectual subjects, map-reading, use of the compass and section formations, were taught by a subaltern of more recent vintage. On the credit side he found he was able to assimilate the rudiments of drill and the intricacies of the Bren gun at a considerably faster rate than his younger contemporaries. This brought rapid success in the Army Cadet Forces' examinations. He passed Parts 1 and 2 of Certificate A and was awarded a chevron. Followed, in rapid succession, by two more. Less congenial were Annual Camps. The food was filling but nondescript. Twelve Cadets, sleeping on straw palliasses laid on duckboards, with their feet towards the centre pole of a bell tent, contrasted unfavourably with home comforts. The contrast was sharpened when it rained and the duckboards sank into the mud. Byrne was damp, his uniform was damp and his bed was damp. He sometimes wondered whether uncomfortable camps and the evenings spent sloping arms and changing step, when he could have spent more time studying for Higher School Certificate, would prove worthwhile.

The second precaution had needed little planning and had taken much less time. It was common knowledge that soldiers had short hair. The Saturday before reporting for duty that Monday morning he had had a haircut. The barber was a noisy, chatty and cheerful ex-wartime Military Policeman, not totally without tonsorial skills but with an unhappy knack of nicking the ears of any customer who moved his head more than a fraction. In spite of the then current vogue of hair styles requiring long hair, lavish applications of Brylcreem and carefully pressed-in waves, he had still not extended his repertoire beyond short back and sides. It was not surprising his clientele tended to be largely middle-aged. 'No problem now, Sir,' he assured Byrne as his scissors clipped the last lock of hair longer than half an inch. He assured Byrne he was quite certain the Army would welcome such an obviously well-groomed young man into their ranks.

This did not prove to be the case. The first day in His Majesty's Service included a parade for haircuts. The N.C.O.s and the Army barbers did not seem to notice, or apparently care, whether a haircut was needed or not. A haircut was only one small diversion in those first busy days. Only a week later, Byrne's recollections had become blurred. He was issued with various items of clothing. He did remember the abrasive quality of the underwear, only rivalled by the itchiness of the rough khaki shirts. The recruits were double-marched here for medical examinations and there for documentation. He was issued with a rifle and his section was unlucky enough to be given weapons heavily coated in a grease preservative. These required many hours of poking out microscopic amounts of grease with the aid of a matchstick and a piece of rag before passing the minute inspection of the Platoon Corporal

Dress in those early days was a shapeless two-piece overall called denims. Of a colour that could only be described as off-grey, the Platoon of recruits appeared anything but smart as, bare-headed, they doubled round the barracks. Much later in life Byrne wondered how anyone could market perfumes so unglamorously named 'Denim' – clearly no-one who had performed National Service.

Accommodation was in plain one-storey buildings evenly spaced around the sides of the barrack square. They verged on the unattractive during fine weather and totally depressing during wet and cold early mornings. Those unfortunates without the advantage of some grounding in military knowledge rapidly learnt that the barrack square was out of bounds except when drill was being performed. Indeed, even to skirt the square had to be done marching smartly. Officers, rarely seen except at a distance, had to be saluted. Everyone else, except fellow recruits, had to be addressed from a position of rigid attention with either a 'No, Corporal' or 'Yes, Sergeant', depending on the rank of the person in question. For several days these two phrases were all that were necessary for recruits to converse with their superiors. Errors on the part of the former were almost always corrected by the latter with a torrent of traditional abuse.

The barrack blocks each held one Platoon. Metal beds, metal lockers and a coke stove in the centre of the room were the sum total of the furnishings. The floors were wooden, two inch wide strips of wood that ran lengthways down the room, still gleaming from the efforts of the previous occupants. The Corporal in charge of the block was a quick-tempered and noisy Ulsterman of apparently no particular military ability but with a natural flair for keeping out of trouble. This included the ability to leave the Corporals' Mess most nights very late, much the worse for wear, unsteadily make his way into his small room at the end of the block with much stumbling and cursing, yet appear with his battledress creased and his boots shining the following morning. His assistant, a large and amicable Lance Corporal with a much friendlier disposition but totally lacking in ambition, though never voicing disapproval, was clearly embarrassed by his senior's conduct.

There was little doubt the aim of the training was to keep the conscripts busy from early dawn, 5.30 a.m., till long past dusk. If one of the objects was to keep them out of trouble, it succeeded. Drill, weapon and physical training were followed by more of the same, day after day. Byrne amazed himself at the feats of agility he could perform which he had tended to avoid in the gym at school. Under the strident urging of the instructors in their red and black striped jerseys the unfit became fit. Tall and fairly heavily built, Byrne had found that climbing a rope at school had always been something of a stately progress. Now he found it easy. Whether it was fear of retribution or of appearing inadequate or ridiculous in front of their peers, the shortest, fattest and weakest drove themselves rapidly to the top of the rope.

There were many other devices to fill in those parts of the sixteen-hour day when the recruits were not being shouted at on the square or were mastering firing positions with a rifle. Cleaning boots and pressing uniforms were only highlights of the supposedly off-duty hours. Frequent kit inspections required every man to lay out every item issued to him on or in front of his bed. From boots to beret and from shining mess tins to sheets, neatly wrapped round with blankets; all had to be arranged in immaculate condition in the approved manner. One sock slightly out of place could result in the painstakingly laid out kit being swept on to the floor and a re-inspection of the whole platoon some hours later.

Black-leading the coke-burning stove and whitening the surrounds required little skill. Requiring a little more skill but considerably more patience was the close attention that had to be paid to three particular two inch strips of flooring. These ran the length of the barrack block in front of the two rows of uncomfortable metal beds set back against the walls. This meant that the occupier of each bedspace was the unfortunate possessor of several feet of three two inch strips for which he was personally responsible. Any spare minutes during the evening were spent black boot polishing the centre of the three strips and scraping those on either side with a razor blade. Painstaking and backbreaking work resulted in a shiny black strip artistically set off by virtually white strips on either side. The overall effect was presumably meant to produce a pleasing contrast with the remainder of the brown highly polished floor. Needless to say, the artistic nuances were largely lost on Byrne and his fellow floor scrapers.

Meal times were regarded as a welcome break in the routine but little more. The recruits were a mixture of ex-Public, Grammar and Secondary Modern School pupils. Some, the local Police had been glad to see leave for the Army, others were resentful at leaving behind a well-paid job; most were resigned to their fate. However, if there was one matter on which an ill-assorted group of eighteen-year-olds could agree, it was on the sheer awfulness of the food, which verged on the inedible. Food was queued for and served in a large inhospitable concrete-floored shed. Meals were dished out by apparently uninterested cooks, grubbily attired. Vegetables were served from what appeared to be old-fashioned wash tubs. The standard method of dispensing the contents was for the cook to use a long-handled scoop and rap the spoon on the tub edge. Meanwhile the recruit hopefully manoeuved his plate underneath, aiming to intercept the food in its rapid downward flight. The little piles of over-cooked cabbage on the ground were evidence of an occasional lack of success. There was a NAAFI but it was of little use during the first few weeks for two reasons. Pay for National Servicemen was low, reduced even further by minor deductions for military purposes which were only partially understood by the raw recruits. Secondly, even those with money found little time to spare from cleaning, polishing, scraping floorboards and pressing uniforms to seek out the traditional char and wads.

Little was seen of the Officers, other than on more formal Platoon and Company Parades. What they did the rest of the time was a mystery to the recruits, though they had little time to speculate on the subject and were little interested. Clearly the training of recruits was something to be almost entirely left to the Warrant Officers and N.C.O.s. During the first two weeks of training, Byrne could recall only being spoken to once by an Officer. He had found time to scribble a few lines home. It was when he had finished that a tiny drop of ink found its way, via his finger, onto his cap badge as he was putting on his beret. 'Verdigris on his cap badge, Sir!' bawled the Sergeant as Byrne stood rigidly to attention in front of the Company Commander's desk. It appeared this was prejudicial to several things, including good order and military discipline. Byrne was mortified at having to offer what, even to him, seemed to be a feeble excuse. He was even more apprehensive of what punishment he would receive for what sounded, in the stentorian tones of the Sergeant, a most serious breach of the King's Regulations. No doubt convinced as to the unlikelihood of anything polishable being left long enough to accumulate even a hint of verdigris, the Company Commander did not appear to take the incident too seriously. Byrne was doubled out of the office, the relieved recipient of an unrecorded admonishment.

The days passed swiftly, cleaning rifles, firing on the range, taking the Bren gun apart and putting it together again, throwing the regulation number of hand grenades, getting bruised on the assault course, drill and more drill. As they sat in the back of the three-tonners taking them to the railway station, their forty-eight-hour leave passes and their travel warrants in their pockets, even those who had been to boarding school and used to being away from home had never experienced a sweeter moment.

On their return there were examinations to decide on the final destinations of the recruits. These were mostly aptitude tests of manual dexterity. Though Byrne had not applied to join that illustrious Corps, he was told firmly that he had no chance of being accepted by the Royal Electrical and Mechanical Engineers. He had distinguished himself by not passing even the first and most elementary of the tests which was the reassembling of a large and simple dismantled lock. Not only did he put it back together so it wouldn't work but he dropped it on the floor, so extracting a pitying look from the invigilating N.C.O. Byrne's consolation was that few others seemed to have the aptitude necessary for the more technical occupations the Army had on offer. Almost the whole intake was irrevocably bound for the Queen of the Battlefield, the Infantry. To compensate for his lack of technical skill Byrne hoped he had, without being too obvious, demonstrated an uncanny knack of acquiring basic military skills. He had not been asked whether he had been in the Army Cadet Force, nor had he volunteered the information. However, his basic military knowledge had been enough for him to show, in an unassuming manner, that he only needed to be shown a drill movement or be told the name of part of a rifle once in order to remember the essentials. Whether it was this carefully displayed aptitude, that he did obtain a Higher School Certificate, a combination of both or some other less obvious method of selection, Byrne found his name along with fifteen others posted on Orders to report for further training to the Junior N.C.O.s Cadre, following a seventy-two-hour pass. The rest of the Company found themselves posted to their Battalions in the Far East, Middle East, West Germany or places of lesser interest in the United Kingdom. The selected sixteen looked forward with mixed feelings to another few weeks in the Army Basic Training Unit.

Having reported in the evening before the Cadre started, the importance of the occasion was marked by an order for the embronic Lance Corporals to move their beds over to a block on the other side of the square at 8.00 p.m. Having done that, they were to replace them with a similar number of beds from the block they were to occupy. The most intelligent of their number failed to grasp the rationale underlying this order and the two-way procession of beds was observed with much amusement by passers-by on their way to the NAAFI.

The potential Junior N.C.O.s Cadre was far more congenial. Though still considered to be raw, they were treated as at least half-trained soldiers. No longer were they shouted at all the time, no longer had they to scrape floorboards or undergo frequent full kit inspections and best of all, the 5.30 a.m. Reveille was replaced by one at the more civilised time of 6.30 a.m. It was true the food was no better, they still went through the thrice daily routine of grumbling but the training was more interesting and there were opportunities to visit the NAAFI, when they had some money. For the first time since their involuntary enlistment, a team spirit started to emerge – even to the extent of doing homework in the barrack block to prepare themselves for a test the following day. The new subjects included Map and Compass work, Section Leading and how to drill a squad. Their instructors most of the time were two senior Corporals. One was a very likeable Geordie called Whitfield. Corporal Whitfield was a wartime soldier with a genuine interest in the well-being and progress of his charges. The other, Corporal Jackson, was younger, bright and immaculately turned-out but with an inclination towards being a poseur and avoiding work. It was quite obvious to the Cadre that he was quite happy if Corporal Whitfield did most of the work and Corporal Jackson got most of the credit.

It was Byrne's turn to clean the ablutions. Even potential Junior N.C.O.s did not escape such menial duties. Cleaning the latrines was accomplished by liberally throwing around buckets of water in all directions, including at least one into each cubicle. The cubicle doors tended to swing shut so the accepted method was to swing a full bucket of water downwards in a rapid semi-circular manner under the door, which was some eighteen inches above the floor. The result was a thorough soaking of the ancient installation from the lavatory pan up to the tank above. This was followed by energetic attention with a broom. That morning Byrne swung his first bucket vigorously under a door, to be unexpectedly rewarded with a roar of anguish from a previously well-groomed Corporal taking an unofficial break to smoke a cigarette and read the *Daily Mirror*. Byrne thought it wise to make a rapid tactical withdrawal.

After three weeks, promotion to the dizzy heights of a Local Acting Unpaid Lance Corporal was very satisfying. There were privileges. On the occasional visit to the NAAFI they were allowed into that special room reserved for Junior N.C.O.s. The way more recent conscripts, when spoken to, snapped to attention with a 'Yes, Corporal' or 'No, Corporal' was another. Under the unassuming and enthusiastic leadership of Corporal Whitfield, the Cadre had become a team.

Special leave was granted to those required to attend school speech days and collect certificates and prizes. They would return with their Higher School Certificate or other qualification, to be greeted on their return with as much pleasure by Corporal Whitfield as if they had been awarded to himself. It was little wonder the Cadre regarded the little Geordie Corporal with affection.

There was a brief interlude in the training for three of the new Lance Corporals to attend the War Office Selection Board at Barton Stacey. This privilege was for those considered to be potential Officers. Barton Stacey being South of London, the long train journey from the North was broken by an overnight stay in London. The claustrophobic accommodation that night, deep below ground in the tunnels of a transit camp at Goodge Street Underground Station, was an unusual but not very comfortable experience. Wandering round London in the afternoon with very little money in their pockets was dispiriting. They decided that between them they had just enough to buy the cheapest seats for a new show *Reluctant Heroes*, showing at the Whitehall Theatre. In the circumstances they found themselves, this seemed appropriate. Though eventually the show became a long-running success, this did not appear to be the case at the time they presented themselves at the box office, resplendent in best battledresses.

To their surprise, apparently for being in uniform, they were given complimentary tickets for the dress circle. Sitting in a near-empty theatre in an almost empty dress circle, they had no inkling of the success *Reluctant Heroes* was to become.

Lance Corporal Byrne had an early premonition he would pass the Selection Board. A good omen was that the number on the front of his identification vest was 103, the telephone number of his girlfriend. With only temporary problems in giving an impromptu lecture on a matchbox tossed on to the floor by one of the Officers, he satisfied the selectors in the practical tests. Most of these seemed to be variants on the same theme, moving a group of his fellows across an imaginary minefield with the aid of planks, ropes, barrels and a tree branch by a combination of planning, exhortation and physical dexterity. The result was a pass.

The passing-out of the Junior N.C.O.s Cadre on the square during the day was rounded off in the evening with the traditional visit to a local pub. Corporal Whitfield's popularity manifested itself in the number of mild and bitters he was bought. By closing time he was as effusive in singing the praises of his young Local Acting Unpaid Lance Corporals as he was legless. This latter condition posed a serious problem. They were in uniform and in those days Guards were Guards. Everyone was scrutinised carefully before leaving the barracks. A soldier without a sufficiently knife-like crease in his battledress trousers would be told by the Guard Commander to return to his billet to attend to the matter before being allowed out. A soldier trying to enter the barracks the worse for wear might find himself detained while the Orderly Sergeant was sent for. Minimally he would have his name taken with the strong possibility of being paraded before a disapproving Company Commander the following morning.

On this occasion even the most vigilant of Guard Commanders would have failed to notice that in the middle of a squad of Lance Corporals marching smartly through the gates was a small Corporal, firmly supported on both sides, lustily joining in 'Blaydon Races', with his feet busily marching some six inches above the ground.

Training finished, the Lance Corporals were posted. Most were posted to the battalions of their choice. A handful, Byrne among them, were told they were to be posted to Officer Cadet School. They were given various tasks to fill in the time before departure. Some were more interesting than others. They were occasionally given squads of recruits to drill on the sacred barrack square. The least interesting job was supervising the dusting of the corridors in the Officers' Mess. The most interesting job by far was instructing on the 2" Mortar Range. To while away the time between the departure of one batch of recruits and the arrival of the next, Byrne practised on his own. He got considerable satisfaction from dropping a high explosive bomb directly on top of a preselected small bush and impressed himself with the pinpoint accuracy that could be achieved with unlimited practice. He obtained even greater satisfaction in demonstrating his new-found skill to the new recruits. He began to feel like an old soldier.

Thinking back years later, Byrne realised his basic training had been thorough; though irksome in its restrictions and living conditions which sometimes bordered on the uncivilised. It would have been surprising if the training had not been efficient following the recent concentrated experience of World War II and the need to train soldiers as quickly as possible. Accommodation had been bleak, ablutions spartan, pay low and the food occasionally indescribable. So different from the Army in decades to come. Byrne didn't notice many of his fellow conscripts volunteering for a Regular Army career, except for the handful who signed on for the minimum period allowable to qualify earlier for Regular Army rates of pay.

By the end of their training, whether they admitted it or not, the conscript Lance Corporals felt at least some satisfaction in working as a team. In the earlier days there had been some mutual sympathy caused by common misery. Sitting on the end of an uncomfortable bed, cleaning kit, staring at featureless walls and the carpetless brown floor provided ample scope for acute attacks of homesickness. With little to look forward to as far as they could see, with the exception of their first leave, it would not have been surprising if a general sense of grievance had not bound at least some of them together. Later there had come a rarely voiced satisfaction in a drill period well done or even in a kit inspection that had not resulted in yet another being ordered in retribution.

The Junior N.C.O.s Cadre had certainly continued to encourage comradeship in a sense peculiar to the British Army – even a conscript one. There had been a willingness to help each other, a desire to do better on exercises than more senior cadres. Those disgruntled at having their careers and plans disrupted by two years with the Colours found this at least overlaid, if not entirely replaced, by an interest in what they were made to do. It was with mixed feelings that Local Acting Unpaid Lance Corporal Byrne was called to the Orderly Room to collect his Railway Warrant, forty-eight-hour pass and Joining Instructions for Eaton Hall Officer Cadet School near Chester.

Chapter 2

Lance Corporal to Second Lieutenant

Byrne was not altogether surprised when he was documented on arrival at Eaton Hall. The Army seemed to take a continuing interest in his date of birth and his home address. As he had expected, appointment as an Officer Cadet meant he had to remove his stripe. In anticipation, he had already done so. Among the various forms he had to complete and sign was one to the effect that he relinquished any rights and privileges he might have possessed in respect of his previous status in the military hierarchy. There was enough stress on this to make him wonder what those important privileges were that he had unwittingly overlooked.

Eaton Hall itself, in the style of an impressively large railway station, housed some Cadets. Others, including Byrne, lived in single-storey brick huts at the side of a long and impressive drive leading to the well-known Golden Gates. 'Golden Gates' was the name also given to a specially composed Cadet School March. A tune that became engraved on the memories of successive intakes of Cadets by the resident band. Room and kit inspections were few and far between compared with the Basic Training Unit but there was no relaxation on standards of turnout. Boots still had to glisten and battledress blouses and trousers pressed to the highest standards. After many hours of shining their 'best boots' with a liberal application of boot polish, worked into the surface with a rag using the well-known small-circling method, the required gloss was not always achieved. This serious state of affairs necessitated the Cadet resorting to the hot spoon/liquid polish method. If this failed, the help of the Company Storeman was enlisted who, for a modest fee, would undertake to produce boots with a surface which would avoid the wrath of the Sergeant-Major. The standard of cuisine, the Cadets were delighted to find, was an improvement. It would have been surprising if this could have been other-

10

wise. There were plates, knives and forks on the table. The floor of the dining hall was tiled. The NAAFI was also superior, modern and spacious. There were, however, few extra spare minutes to take advantage of the delights on offer.

The weeks at Officer Cadet School were busy with little leave granted and that only for short periods. So short were the leaves that visits home were only rarely worthwhile. That there was little leave and free time generally was certainly because of a pending official visit of Princess Elizabeth. Most, if not all Cadets, were Royalists of varying degrees of enthusiasm. However, even the most loyal of the King's subjects could have been forgiven for occasionally wishing the Princess had chosen an earlier or later date.

During the weeks before the visit, the Guards', Warrant Officers and Drill Sergeants threw themselves into the task of producing an immaculate parade with an awesome enthusiasm. 'Names were taken' liberally. With feverish energy, ferocious commands and threats of dire retribution, a swarm of N.C.O.s under a never-satisfied R.S.M. made life exhausting for the Officer Cadets of Eaton Hall. Whether it arose out of total exasperation, a wicked sense of humour or was simply to impress the Cadets with the punishments that could come their way, the R.S.M. occasionally despatched Sergeants and Warrant Officers alike to report to the Guard Room as a reward for the alleged ineptitude of their Cadets. Byrne and his fellow Cadets eventually produced a standard of drill they realised in later life they would never reach again. It was a great relief to march off after the great day to the then all too familiar strains of 'Golden Gates'.

Life was not all drill. There were lectures and examinations on tactics, giving orders, Army organisations, King's Regulations, mines, barbed wire, vehicle inspections and all the other subjects of which knowledge was essential to an aspiring Platoon Commander. They fired the Vickers Machine Gun and the 3" Mortar. To their regret the Cadets did not get the opportunity to conduct a live artillery shoot. The substitute for this took place on a landscape model mounted on a large piece of hessian which sloped upwards away from the class. An immaculately-clad Gunner Officer, resplendent in breeches and Sam Browne, introduced his lesson with the statement that in the next war their Platoon would be supported by the Royal Regiment of Artillery and if they were lucky, by the Royal Horse Artillery. A piece of blatant one-upmanship which would most certainly have irritated any potential non-R.H.A. Gunners had they been present. Fortunately, Gunners attended the sister O.C.S. at Mons.

When conducting an imaginary shoot and giving directions to an equally imaginary Gun Battery, map references given by the Cadets were registered by a perspiring Gunner under the hessian who would mark the fall of shot with a puff of cigarette smoke at the appropriate place. Less competent Cadets, who used more directions and imaginary shells than strictly necessary in bracketing the target, undoubtedly contributed to the Gunner's smoker's cough.

Exercises in the Welsh mountains were often hard and demanding. Winter made them doubly so. The hardest lesson to learn was patience. Two and three-day exercises were largely brief periods of inactivity and much longer ones of monotony. The monotony was often aggravated by extreme cold and snow or cold and rain. It was difficult, if not impossible, to maintain potential officer-like enthusiasm while sitting for hours on end in an icy slit trench in the early hours of the morning.

If the aim of the training in the Welsh mountains was to make anything that followed on active service at least bearable, it succeeded. Byrne remembered one particularly cold and dark night in which he was fortunately, as it turned out, acting as a humble rifleman. His Platoon had been detailed to produce a Fighting Patrol and to snatch a prisoner or two from the opposition. The patrol had been carefully briefed, under the eagle eyes of the Directing Staff, on compass bearings, passwords, the prominent features they would encounter and the number of steps they would be taking on the different legs of the approach to the enemy lines. With few responsibilities other than to follow the man in front, after more than an hour of careful approach work, Byrne suspected the patrol was lost. He got the firm impression that they had set off correctly enough but for some reason had gone off on a tangent to the left and then swung to the right in a semicircle. It was far too dark for the ground features to be of any use at all. Under the conditions, success in finding the enemy's position depended entirely on accurate compass work and counting paces carefully. Something was seriously amiss. The patrol was still under the scrutiny of the ever-present umpires who most assuredly had formed the opinion that the only positive outcome of this particular patrol was to allow the acting Platoon Commander and Sergeant to learn from their mistakes. The Cadets plodded along quietly with dogged determination, though where to by now was a mystery.

Uncertainty was abruptly removed when, one by one, the patrol silently walked over the edge of a small cliff to land on top of each other some ten feet below. Discipline held. There were no cries of pain, even though there was a liberal sprinkling of bruises and sprains among the now battered Fighting Patrol as they slowly started to disentangle themselves from each other and their rifles and Sten guns. As if this catastrophe wasn't enough, there was a further indignity yet to come. Unwittingly, the Patrol had managed to thread their way through the enemy's position from the rear before falling over the edge. To their embarrassment, the enemy lined the top of the cliff and offered unsolicited comments on the tactical abilities of their opponents and ribald advice in general. Further to this, under the circumstances, they were all dead. Withdrawing with as much dignity as possible under the circumstances, which was very little, was the only course open.

Battle Camp was viewed with both trepidation and anticipation. The Camp was held at Okehampton at the end of their training. It was two weeks of intense exercises at Section, Platoon and Company level. A satisfactory performance was necessary to pass out. An unsatisfactory performance could result in having to repeat the fortnight or even being 'returned to unit' uncommissioned. During the weeks of training some Cadets had been returned to their units without fuss. Such happenings were noticed but simply not discussed. For those remaining, the thought of failing at this last hurdle was too much to contemplate. Successful Cadets returning from their fortnight on Dartmoor naturally embellished the horrors of the experience for the benefit of those next to go. On the train to Okehampton, Byrne and his fellow Cadets, though inwardly full of apprehension, were determined to pass this last test if it were humanly possible.

Dartmoor was not too forbidding in the early Spring. As always, in spite of the warm weather and sunshine, much of the moor was wet; not that there was much time to admire the scenery. The accommodation was in Nissen huts, sparsely furnished with bedsteads and lockers and there was the inevitable concrete floor. The Cadets left early in the morning for exercises and usually returned late at night.

A particularly exacting and oft-repeated test was leading a section across the moor when rifle or automatic fire would be directed at them from varying distances, positions and directions. The bullets were not actually aimed at them but uncomfortably close enough to catch their attention.

Exercise followed exercise. There were Section, Platoon and Company Battle Drills. Left flanking and right flanking movements and frontal assaults followed each other in quick succession. The Cadets took it in turns to act as Section and Platoon Commanders and all the other jobs that made up these minor formations. One tactical situation was followed by another. The embryonic officers quickly learnt the importance of rapid and preferably sensible decisions; though a half-wrong decision taken quickly was considered better than a correct one taken too late. Was the answer to use fire and movement to flank the enemy or was a courageous frontal assault called for? Was there an even more effective solution with which to impress the Directing Staff?

Platoon attacks almost invariably involved using the 2" Mortar to fire either smoke or high explosive bombs, or both, at the enemy's position. Smoke was to hide their own movements and high explosive to keep the enemy's heads down until the assault was upon them. When the order came for the 2" Mortarmen to move forward and do their stuff, a modicum of prestige could be earned from the speed with which they responded and the number and accuracy of the bombs they could get into the air at the same time. Cadet Lewis, acting N.C.O. i/c Mortar, was anxious to create a favourable impression and persuaded his team, of which Byrne was one, to carry three times the usual number of mortar bombs that morning. The expected need for the 2" Mortar did not materialise as early as expected and the Mortarmen, sweating profusely, were by no means sure Cadet Lewis's idea was going to turn out to be such a good one after all. There were several attacks of a minor nature on the Platoon as it made its way forward. None of these, in the judgement of the Platoon Commander, required the services of the 2" Mortar to repel; much to Byrne's disappointment.

It was not until five weary miles had been covered in the warm sun that their time came. The Platoon was fired on by the enemy, estimated to be of section strength, from the forward slope of a small hill 400 yards away. The leading section showed itself off, for the benefit of the Directing Staff, with some smartly conducted fire and movement manoeuvres and then went to ground. They were, so they were informed, under effective fire and could go no further. The Platoon Commander, in the approved manner, made an appreciation of the situation and formed a plan. The decision was to left flank the enemy with the remaining two sections while the section already pinned down provided supporting fire. An essential part of the plan was for the 2" Mortar to fire high explosive to keep the enemy's heads down and smoke to cover the movement of the riflemen in the final assault. Cadet Lewis and his Mortarmen received the order to move forward into a firing position with joy in their hearts. They doubled forward and piled their bombs, determined that the fastest and densest mortar stonk ever seen on Dartmoor was about to be fired. The order came to fire and the first bomb was already sliding down the barrel when the Directing Staff called a halt. Sheep had been seen wandering across the area in the direction of the enemy's hill. In deference to Range Standing

Orders, the Mortar bombardment would have to be taken as read. With heavy hearts and equally heavy loads in prospect, the Mortar crew repacked the bombs into their containers and prepared to sprint forward when the enemy's position was taken and they were signalled to regroup on the far side.

There were no further calls for the 2" Mortar. Some ten miles and more and several hours later, it was totally exhausted and much wiser Officer Cadets that staggered into the ammunition store to return the unused bombs.

The end of the first week was nearing when disaster struck. The previous evening Byrne had stood on a nail. It had penetrated through the sole of his boot into his left foot. He washed and disinfected what he thought was a minor wound and thought little of it at the time. The following day, not only was the foot very painful but it had swollen hugely. Not able to put on his boot, he had no option but to attend sick parade that morning. He was well aware of the implications – the possibility of being unable to complete the second week which would inevitably mean repeating the whole nerve-wracking fortnight.

Byrne hobbled painfully into the Medical Inspection Room and reported to the Orderly. The Medical Officer was summoned and he was in no doubt as to the treatment required. Rest and being bedded down in Camp was out of the question. The infected foot needed drug treatment and almost certainly a long period of recuperation. The doctor made some notes, a telephone call to the hospital and an ambulance was summoned to take a self-pitying Byrne to the Royal Naval Hospital in Plymouth. On arrival and after another examination, he was wheeled along endless corridors and put to bed. It appeared his elevated status as an Officer Cadet entitled him to a large dark-brown and dismal room. He was left to his own devices. Not that there was anything to do or anyone to talk to; the Navy was obviously a healthy Service as the hospital seemed short of customers.

Apart from meals brought by an orderly, his only visitor was an uncommunicative and cheerless nursing sister who every few hours stuck a hypodermic needle unceremoniously into his buttocks. After initial embarrassment, Byrne soon got used to lowering his pyjama trousers and presenting his bare bottom to a lady. The treatment was as effective as it was undignified and the pain and swelling rapidly started to subside. However, the longer term medical outlook was not hopeful. The most optimistic forecast the doctor allowed himself was discharge at the end of the following week. Just in time, Byrne calculated, to return to Eaton Hall and watch the passing-out parade instead of taking part. The prospect of a second Battle Camp seemed as inevitable as it was unwanted.

By the following Monday his foot was still a little sore but much nearer normal size. Byrne decided decisive action was called for; he discharged himself. He packed his uniform, avoided the reception area and signed himself out at the Guardroom. No-one asked him any questions and Byrne did not volunteer that the only authority for his seemingly innocent departure was his own. Clearly, patients walking out of Military Hospitals without permission was not an occurrence that normally had to be guarded against. He harboured no illusions of heroism and had not weighed the possible consequences of his actions. A desperate but almost certainly hopeless attempt to avoid another Battle Camp was uppermost in his mind. Having got so far, the prospects of another two weeks or more seemed like an eternity. He hitch-hiked to the Camp at Okehampton, somewhat naively expecting any minute that a Military Police road block would stop the vehicle and he would be taken back to hospital under arrest.

It was late afternoon when he reached his hut. On their return that evening, his exhausted fellow Cadets were too tired to take more than a polite and desultory interest in his reappearance. Early the following day he paraded with the rest and reported to the Company Commander. Some soreness had returned and his limp was not entirely an old soldier's ploy. The Company Commander cut short his carefully rehearsed explanation and as Byrne expected, he was immediately sent to the M.I. Room. He knew he had no option but to tell the whole story to the Medical Officer. He was certain it would only be a matter of hours before any departure from the truth would be detected. He was equally convinced that deception would enhance whatever awful retribution that was likely to come his way from the military authorities. Making sure he stressed his keenness to return to his Company rather than any other motive, he confessed all. Inwardly he cursed his foot, bad luck and above all, his crass stupidity in getting himself into such a mess.

To his surprise and relief the M.O. found his story mildly amusing. Having examined the offending foot, he pronounced it on the mend. Three days light duties and 'excused boots' were ordered. No mention was made of disciplinary proceedings arising from his precipitate and unauthorised departure from the Royal Naval Hospital. By the time the examination was over the Cadets had long departed to the moors for another day of toil. He was left to his own thoughts for the rest of the day. These were tinged with apprehension. He had yet to face the Company Commander. That evening he visited the Church Army hut for a cup of tea and joined in a hymn.

Next day he paraded again, embarrassed at wearing shoes which con-trasted oddly with his steel helmet and rifle. After the parade he was summoned into the imposing presence of the Company Commander. He found he was a minor hero. It appeared he had exhibited that indefinable quality essential to any Officer Cadet, 'moral fibre'. Conduct that would have been considered in civilian life to be at the least unwise, was not so in the Army. His obvious desire to return to duty as soon as possible, regardless of the consequences, was commendable. The Company Com-mander urged the other Cadets to follow this example. Byrne momentarily basked with suitable modesty in this unexpected and undeserved glory. His fellow Cadets, who were not gullible, did not wholeheartedly indulge in the uncritical hero-worship urged upon them.

The question remained as to what Byrne was to do for the next three days before he was returned to full duties. His Company Commander decided that he should be his personal assistant. The duties were simple. He was required to follow the Company Commander around and carry a small notebook. In this he would make such entries as the Major thought fit to dictate. To supplement this onerous chore, Byrne thought it advis-able to join the Directing Staff from time to time in cheering the efforts of the Cadets and loudly exhorting them to even greater exertions on the assault course and during the other activities designed to produce leader-ship, teamwork and physical fitness.

He enjoyed the three days of medical restriction for the most part, though he sometimes felt a trifle guilty when his Platoon got particularly well-soaked and covered in mud. These feelings were reinforced when he was obliged to acknowledge Officers' instructions to be careful, take things easily and to rest his foot whenever he thought it necessary; espe-cially when he was conscious his foot had, for all practical purposes, healed. He also had to endure in the evening the occasional half-meant envious and sarcastic comments of his peers. Not that he really minded this slightly less than sympathetic treatment, the nightmarish prospect of another Battle Camp had disappeared. Good things came to an end when, for the last few days, he returned to normal duties and had to take extra turns acting as Section or Platoon Commander to make up for what he had missed. Byrne survived the ordeal without serious mishap. A successful Battle Camp was completed. No-one was returned to his unit or required to undergo the Dartmoor experience a second time.

It was a very happy group of Officer Cadets that returned to Eaton Hall. There was much polishing of best boots and pressing of battledresses ready for the final passing-out parade in front of admiring parents and girlfriends. There was more of the inevitable documentation and news of their postings. It was no surprise to Byrne, as he had included the Yorkshire Fusiliers in his list of choices, to find that he had been commissioned into his County Regiment and posted to the 1st Battalion in Malaya. It was also only then that he became conscious that a war had started in that part of the world, though he was not entirely sure when it had started, by whom or what it was all about. In any case there was too much to do at Eaton Hall without worrying overmuch about the future.

The Company of Officer Cadets formed up in review order, marched past to the strains of 'Golden Gates' and then off the square for the last time at Light Infantry pace. Byrne enjoyed his embarkation leave.

Second Lieutenant Byrne was directed to report to the Officers' Mess where he had once supervised the cleaning of the corridors. He was due to spend one night there before continuing his journey to the Far East. Any nostalgic inclinations he might have had to look up old friends or enemies were thwarted by the attentions of the M.O. It was the Doctor's duty to protect him against Blackwater Fever, Yellow Fever and a host of other afflictions that would beset soldiery in the ports of call on the way to Singapore. The M.O. spoke nothing but the truth when he said the prophylactic treatment would hurt Byrne more than it would hurt him.

Early the next morning Byrne was taken to the railway station with twenty other National Servicemen. A few hours later they found themselves on a quay beside the River Mersey looking up at the troopship *Empire Comet* towering above them.

Chapter 3

The Mersey to Malaya

The Troopship *Empire Comet* was closely packed with soldiers. They were mainly reinforcements or replacements for Battalions and Regiments already in Malaya and Korea. Second Lieutenant Byrne's draft of National Service Yorkshire Fusiliers was allocated its place on a crowded lower mess deck. Byrne himself, with the privilege of rank, was given the uppermost of two bunks in a tiny bare cabin which he shared with an equally brand-new subaltern in the Gunners. Being keen, he determined to put into practice, as soon as possible, the skills in man-management he had been taught at Officer Cadet School. At this early stage in his military career they were almost entirely theoretical. Eaton Hall had not provided soldiers on whom to practise. Cajoling fellow Cadets had not been the same thing. If they had been in a co-operative mood everything went well. If, good-humouredly, they decided to vary somewhat their interpretation of a perfectly clear tactical order, it was usually not too difficult for an acting Platoon Commander to persuade an experienced Directing Staff that any resulting non-textbook manoeuvres were not entirely his fault. On the whole, the Cadets had made things work for each other, well aware their turn in the hot seat would come.

With a long sea voyage in prospect, it was not coping with matters tactical that concerned Byrne. Clearly the emphasis had to be on looking after the welfare of his men. Unfortunately, his good intentions were not to be put into practice for very many days to come. The aches in the places where the Medical Officer had practised his art of preventing him catching horrific diseases had caused acute discomfort. The pain was subsiding and this was not his worry. He had known from an early age he was not destined to be a sailor. Certainly not a sailor who travelled in comfort. He remembered occasional sea fishing trips in small boats off the coast of

Whitby when he had accompanied his Father. These had always resulted in bouts of seasickness which even success with rod and line had done little to assuage. Standing on the deck watching Birkenhead and Liverpool fade away as the ship left the calm waters of the estuary, naively, it turned out, he comforted himself with the belief that seasickness was largely a psychological phenomenon. In any case, he reasoned a large ship was a very different proposition from a small fishing boat.

As the ship reached open sea, though there was only a slight chop on the sea, he was sick; very sick. A few others felt rather unwell. Byrne felt dreadful. Immediately his life started to revolve, an apposite word, around his cabin and the antiseptic unwelcoming ablutions next door. He became all too familiar with both. Much of the time he felt death would have been a merciful release. Officers and men who had been absent from meals during the first day or so started to present themselves for refreshment, appetites heightened because of their enforced lack of nourishment. It was not until the *Empire Comet* was sailing past the Rock of Gibraltar that Byrne made his way, still unsteadily, into the dining room for a light breakfast. Unfamiliar to the other diners, his arrival created a mild interest, particularly among the more well-travelled officers, as to where he had come from. No-one even contemplated that it was possible to be sick from Liverpool all the way into the Mediterranean in fine weather. To his relief, Byrne found the same number of soldiers in his draft as there were when he shepherded them aboard at Birkenhead. They seemed none the worse for the enforced lack of officer-interest in their welfare.

He liked the Mediterranean. He liked the sun, the gentle warmth, the blue sea and particularly the entire absence of waves. It was as well he had recovered as minor duties began to come his way. These included paying the troops. He was given a mess deck to pay, a large amount of money in a bag and a sheaf of forms. Byrne was flattered yet slightly apprehensive at the trust the Ship's Paymaster put in him. Fortunately he remembered being shown the forms at O.C.S. In theory they presented little difficulty, requiring only that the amount of money shown by each name was paid out and a signature obtained. Sitting at a table piled with money in the middle of a crowded Mess Deck he thought mistakes would be inevitable. With the help of the N.C.O. in charge he started. When he finally ran out of money, everyone had been paid and the completed paperwork met with the satisfaction of the Paymaster. There was plenty of time left to lean over the ship's rail and admire the shining blue sea. Life was pleasant.

The *Empire Comet* anchored off Port Said before entering the Suez Canal and there was shore leave for some. Even before this was organised, the gully-gully men came on board and the ship was surrounded by bumboats. The troops admired the gully-gully men who produced small chicks from the ears and clothing of their audience with astonishing dexterity. In spite of being warned, many bought cheap leather wallets decorated with crudely coloured maps of Egypt. Though they had been assured they were of the highest quality, they quickly started to fall apart when the stitching gave way as the voyage progressed. Senior Officers continued to warn, without success, against the buying of inferior souvenirs from the boats that crowded round the sides of the ship. To those who went ashore the impression was one of squalor. No-one was too sorry when the ship left Port Said and entered the Suez Canal.

It was hot as they sailed through the Suez Canal. Whatever they had been expecting, it was an anticlimax. There was little scenery to admire. In front of them stretched a straight waterway. Behind them was the same and on either side there was the brown sand of the desert under the oppressive sun. Even the games of housey-housey, one day to sweep the U.K. as bingo, run by the senior warrant officer, lost their attraction and became listless, poorly attended affairs. The only pastime for the soldiers was to lean over the rails and greet the occasional groups of British troops they saw sitting on the canal bank. From the safety of the ship they would shout 'Get your knees brown!' The crude reactions of those on the receiving end of this devastating witticism showed that such advice was not appreciated, particularly by those undergoing an unenviable Canal Zone posting from those who had barely started to get even the slightest tinge of brown on their own knees.

There was a brief stop at Aden and the *Empire Comet* headed towards Ceylon. Away from the heat of the Canal, the temperature in the evening became less overpowering. The Senior Officer on the ship, a Colonel of Engineers, decided the troops should be kept active with some organised sport. An evening's inter-Regimental boxing competition was decreed to keep the troops entertained. The competition was not to be the usual amateur three rounds of three minutes each round. It was to be a mill, where two boxers fought each other for two or three minutes, they then ducked out of the ring to be replaced by two more and so on. The aim was non-stop action and maximum participation. Byrne put the competition details to his twenty Yorkshire Fusiliers. With few exceptions their reactions lacked enthusiasm. Few had boxed before and the remainder showed no inclination to start learning, especially in public. Remembering lessons learnt, Byrne appealed to Regimental pride. Were the Yorkshire Fusiliers afraid of the Glosters or the Royal Northumberland Fusiliers? After all, it was only for three minutes. As a loyal Fusilier, he found himself saying, he would volunteer to be a team member. This inspired piece of leadership worked and a reluctant team was produced. He felt an inner glow of satisfaction as he submitted the official Yorkshire Fusilier team list and weights to the organising officers. He comforted himself that, even though his boxing experience had been confined to a few rounds of very friendly sparring at school and in the A.C.F., he should be able to avoid getting hurt during three minutes. His opponent might even be smaller and less experienced than he was.

Later that day he began to wonder whether he had been entirely wise in his officer-like determination to lead from the front. The organiser, an Army Physical Training Corps Captain, said that he had examined all the lists and matched the contestants by weight. It was most unfortunate that there appeared to be no other competitor of the same weight or even the same height to match him. Byrne was over six feet and weighed over twelve stones. The organiser was extremely sorry but he would not be able to include him in the evening's proceedings. Would Byrne mind finding a substitute for himself? Byrne outwardly expressed disappointment at being unable to take part but under the circumstances he would reluctantly look for a substitute.

The enthusiastic A.P.T.C. Officer hadn't quite finished. He had naturally realised how disappointed Byrne would be at not taking part, so he had arranged for a special three-round exhibition match to conclude the evening's entertainment. His opponent would be another Officer. Although he was well over a stone heavier than Byrne it was, after all, only an exhibition match. Byrne was certainly not convinced that he should welcome this unexpected turn of events but had no alternative but to agree with seeming enthusiasm to the arrangements so kindly made on his behalf.

It was a still, warm, tropical evening. There were bright stars in the dark sky. Byrne's attention was not on the beauties of Nature but on the floodlit boxing ring surrounded by cheering troops. He could see why the event was called a mill. Little physical damage was done but the flailing arms did resemble windmills out of control. Dozens of boxers from different Regiments, few with even the rudiments of technique, attacked each other with great enthusiasm. To the encouraging shouts of their supporters, pair after pair of boxers ducked into the ring, energetically threw wild punches at each other then ducked out again at the sound of the bell. His mind was not entirely on the fortunes of his men, who acquitted themselves with distinction but without winning any prizes. He had seen his own opponent. The Captain, a Regular and older soldier, was no taller than Byrne but his shoulders were ominously broad. Byrne was not comforted by a rumour circulating in the Yorkshire Fusilier Camp to the effect that he was the current B.A.O.R. Heavyweight Champion. A rumour that proved to be well-founded.

The bouts over, the winners congratulated, the exhibition match was announced. The Champion was introduced to a storm of popular acclaim. His gallant opponent who, so it was said, had willingly volunteered to allow him the opportunity to display his skills, was similarly greeted. Nobody had told Byrne anything about this. The loudest cheering by far was from twenty Yorkshire Fusiliers, ecstatic in anticipation. Byrne had never felt so alone and vulnerable. The first two rounds were fairly painless. He moved swiftly round the ring with his fists in what he hoped were the approved position. He occasionally struck the Champion lightly and received in return slightly harder and more frequent blows on his own person. The whole performance was altogether too gentlemanly. Though he was concentrating as he had rarely done before, he could still sense the audience was finding the bout a good deal less exciting than the earlier non-stop action. In short, they were bored.

At the start of the last round Byrne made a mistake. He received a hard blow to the face. This was in all probability not intended and happened because he had been too slow to move out of the way of an exhibition and well-signalled right cross. This logical explanation did not occur to Byrne at the time. Even though by then his nerve ends had been rendered almost numb, this unexpected blow still hurt. In annoyance he struck the surprised Champion a firm blow on the jaw. He received an equally firm thump on the chest in return. The rest of the round was a battle royal. Byrne attacked with great ferocity and little science, inflicting occasional but only minor damage. In return he was punished heavily by a now irritated opponent. The audience and particularly the delirious Yorkshire Fusiliers, cheered until the final bell.

Being an exhibition match, no winner was declared. Byrne had no doubt who had won. The sheer pain of it all didn't make itself felt until during the seawater shower after the contest when his nerve ends began to function again. The following morning he leant over the ship's rail, parts of his face tender and swollen and felt sorry for himself. His upper body still ached from the previous night's exertions. While he was contemplating the horizon the Colonel of Engineers came over to congratulate him on a plucky performance against a vastly more experienced opponent. For a moment, in his innocence, Byrne wondered if that made the painful episode worthwhile.

There was little to do on the troopship during the day except watch the sea or doze. There was hardly enough room for physical training, even if it hadn't been too hot for anything more than a gentle stroll. The only notable incident was the sighting of sharks which caused a rush on to the deck and a brief flurry of letter writing. The next brief stay and the last port of call before Singapore, was Ceylon. Byrne took the advice of more seasoned travellers, missed out the sights of Colombo and took a short trip up the coast to the Mount Lavinia Hotel. From there he was able to write home for the first time about palm trees, golden sands and the blue sea. He sat on the patio, sipping tea and resisting the persuasion of those offering immensely valuable precious stones at ridiculously cheap prices. He watched the more affluent of the local inhabitants at play on the shore and envied the exotic meals and wines being prepared for them at prices he could not afford.

The *Empire Comet* cruised down the Straits of Malacca. For the first time the Malaya-bound National Service Yorkshire Fusiliers every now and again could make out the indefinable smell of the jungle. An aroma with which, in a short time, they would become all too familiar. The *Empire Comet* docked in the busy port of Singapore. There was no time to explore the appetising smells of the Chinese restaurants or the myriad of small shops. Byrne handed over his draft to a Senior N.C.O. to be taken to the Battalion. He had got to know those he had come to regard as his soldiers well during the long voyage and later he was disappointed to find that none of them had been earmarked for C Company. An Officer from the Battalion, awaiting transport to the U.K., had been detailed to meet him as his final duty. Byrne's not very bulky kit was loaded on to a lorry for the railway station. There was just time for a virtually obligatory cup of tea in the Raffles Hotel – 'At least you can say you've been there,' said the U.K.-bound Officer. Sipping tea, served by immaculately white-clad waiters on pure white tablecloths, with the tables placed on an equally immaculate green lawn, was to be a far cry from what was to come.

Over tea, his fellow officer was able to brief him on matters of mundane but vital importance. Byrne had many questions. His joining instructions from the Adjutant of the Battalion had been copious both in detail and length. The Adjutant had recommended the buying of several items of clothing and equipment. The imposing missive had not arrived in sufficient time to allow all of the purchases to be made. In retrospect it appeared this was fortunate. He was relieved to hear that both saddlery and suitable clothing for attending the Singapore Races were most unlikely to be needed. He was confidently assured that opportunities both to ride, play polo and to attend race meetings were non-existent. Byrne wondered if the joining instructions were a relic of pre-W.W.II days when the Battalion was stationed in peace time India.

Before boarding the up-country night train, each of the soldiers was issued with a rifle and two clips holding ten rounds of ammunition. Being issued with live rounds of ammunition on a civilian railway station was the first inkling that, whatever was happening in Malaya, it was not a phoney war. Byrne was allocated a top sleeping berth in a dingy and spartan sleeping compartment. He had had a long and tiring day in the humidity of Singapore. Lying down to test the unyielding mattress, he noticed an irregular line of five small holes in the side of the carriage by his head, through which he could see the lights of the station platform. The jagged edges were bent towards him. He feared to ask. Making what he hoped sounded like a casual enquiry, he was told by the Chinese attendant that the holes were the result of the train being fired upon two days before. Making sure his loaded rifle was within easy reach, he settled down to an uneasy sleep on the hard mattress, comforting himself that lightning did not strike twice in the same place. The journey was bumpy and long. It was hot in the coach. The train stopped at intervals. Each time he woke up, wondering if the next thing he would hear would be shots followed by vicious slaps as bullets penetrated the thin shell of the carriage. After a while, as no-one else seemed worried about the frequent halts, Byrne fell into a fitful sleep.

He was not sorry when, in glorious morning sunshine, he arrived at Kuala Gajah station. He was met by a Battalion H.Q. Land Rover complete with driver and escort to take him to Battalion Headquarters. Headquarters was not far from the railway station. It was housed, together with Support Company, which comprised the Machine Gun and Mortar Platoons, in a well laid out and spacious camp. Green jungle-covered hills surrounded the camp on three sides and it was only a mile away from the nearest major town. Enclosed by barbed wire with cleared fields of fire, it was not surprising the camp had not been attacked. As he was driven through the gates, Byrne saw the 3" Mortar Platoon exercising itself firing bombs on to the surrounding slopes – to keep in practice, with always the chance of providing a nasty shock for any bandits observing troop movements, he was later told. There was a brief welcome from the Commanding Officer and a somewhat frosty one from the Adjutant but no extensive briefing on the Battalion's Company positions. As Byrne was to find out, such information would have been 'nice to know' but would not have been in the 'need to know' category. This was a Platoon and Section

Commanders' war, where the bigger picture could be left to senior officers
as it rarely affected directly day-to-day small scale operations. From the
ordinary soldier's viewpoint, what really mattered was what the Platoon
was doing the following day, for how long and was the day off that had
been rumoured still on for Monday week?

It took rather less than two days in Battalion Headquarters for Byrne to
be completely kitted out. He was issued with his working clothes. These
included 'jungle greens', lace-up canvas boots, floppy green hat, a set of
webbing and a machete. The last-mentioned was a large knife complete
with sheath for cutting through the jungle – an ill-balanced and not very
useful tool which Byrne found few carried. Much more useful was the
poncho. This invaluable item was a large-size groundsheet with a hole for
the head in the middle, complete with drawstring. The local Regimental
Tailors, three industrious Indian contractors, produced overnight made-
to-measure green uniform tunics and shorts. On the instructions of the
Adjutant, for more formal wear, the tailors produced a white mess jacket,
a cummerbund in the Regimental Colours plus some lightweight suiting.
The speed at which they worked was something Byrne had never seen and
never would again. He wondered, as he re-packed his suitcases, how many
opportunities he would actually get to wear the expensive white and shiny
sharkskin dinner jacket; a last minute addition to his wardrobe that the
Adjutant had strongly advised he should have made for dining out on
formal civilian occasions.

There was just time to write two hurried, ten cents each Forces Mail
letters home before a truck arrived from C Company. It came with two
escorts plus a Humber Scout Car sporting two Bren Guns on the mounting
in front of the top hatch. Feeling, for the first time, distinctly warlike and
military, Byrne took his place beside the truck driver, clipped a magazine
on to his carbine, cocked the weapon, applied the safety catch and pointed
the weapon in the approved manner at the surrounding countryside. The
small convoy moved off.

The thirty miles to C Company Headquarters were covered at a brisk
pace. It was Byrne's first opportunity to take a closer look at the countryside which was to be his home for the next year and a half. Just in case, he
clutched his American M1 carbine tightly, particularly when passing
through defiles. It was not difficult to imagine bandits laying in wait
among the green undergrowth which fringed the tops of the steep brown
sides, their fingers ready, crooked round triggers.

Much of the tarmac road to C Company passed through less threatening
surroundings. He saw massive grey water buffaloes, paddy fields, wooden

houses on stilts and little brown children playing. He admired the colourful sarongs of what appeared to him to be uniformly beautiful Malay women. In small villages, industrious Chinese went about their business, some on their bicycles, others semi-running carrying heavy loads. There were rubber plantations. From a distance, to Byrne's Yorkshire eye, they looked as well-groomed as cricket pitches, if it were not for the rubber trees standing in impeccably straight lines. Here and there a few rubber tappers moved rapidly from tree to tree, taking the small pot of liquid latex from its holder and emptying it into the container on their backs, then cutting a new swathe of wood from the descending spiralling groove on the tree to cause the latex to flow again. Other plantations were unkempt and overgrown. Some to the point of appearing almost impenetrable with only narrow tracks winding among the undergrowth from tree to tree. Towering over everything was the jungle, tree-covered hill upon hill as far as the eye could see, until they faded in the distant haze.

The truck and scout car swung off the road. A soldier at the entrance to the camp slapped his rifle butt in salute and the small part that 2Lt. Byrne was to play in the Malayan Emergency had begun.

Chapter 4

First Patrol

The Commander and the Second-in-Command of C Company were war-time soldiers, both of whom had held more senior ranks at the end of the last war. They did not appear to resent their enforced drop in rank, being only too grateful to find a worthwhile job in a smaller postwar Army. They greeted Byrne's arrival with enthusiasm. It appeared, apart from the fact a new face was always welcome in an isolated station, that replacement Platoon Commanders were not always available when they were needed.

The Platoon Commanders were National Servicemen. The Company Commander told Byrne he was to take over 8 Platoon in a few days time from a Subaltern due to return to the U.K. That afternoon he met the Platoon; twenty-one National Servicemen, two of them Lance Corporals, plus one Regular Corporal and a Platoon Sergeant. With memories of lessons in Infantry Battalion establishments still fresh in his mind, Byrne knew this was well under the approved Platoon strength. However, as he was to find out, 8 Platoon was little different from the rest of the platoons in the Battalion and more importantly, a larger platoon would only rarely have been an advantage.

The members of 8 Platoon certainly appeared to be seasoned veterans dressed in their jungle-greens, carefully cleaning and oiling what appeared at first glance to be a bewildering array of weapons. They wore their jungle hats according to individual taste. This varied widely, from imitations of the Australian bush hat to the shapeless, with a wavy brim turned down all the way round. Though they looked veterans, the records in the Company Office showed that, with the exception of the Regular Soldiers, Sergeant Lennox and Corporal Grice, in their mid-twenties, no soldier in 8 Platoon was more than eighteen months older than Byrne himself. Their service with the Company varied from a few weeks to eighteen months.

The Company was located in what was reputed to be active bandit country in North Johore, not far from a large village. The Platoon lived in two rows of dark brown ridge tents between those of 7 and 9 Platoons. Army-issue metal beds, duckboards and lockers made up the total furniture of each tent. The Company base was on the site of a prewar disused plantation medical centre. Three old wooden buildings remained and these were used as a cookhouse/dining room, stores/armoury and Officers' Mess respectively. The combined Company Office, Operations wireless room, Sergeants' Mess, Charwallah's Canteen and other activities essential to the well being of an operational Infantry Company, were housed in larger tents.

Home comforts were few. There was no Company cinema and there was no question of visiting any local places of entertainment – even if they had existed. Indeed, the local village had no outwardly visible tourist attractions. It did boast a station which was on the main railway line from Singapore to the North, with which Byrne was to become well acquainted. Even if the troops had been allowed to visit the township, which they weren't, it was doubtful whether any would have bothered. Drinking water had to be brought daily by water-truck, driven by the indefatigable Private Gingell, from a nearby Dunlop plantation. On the credit side, the soldiers' laundry was done quickly and efficiently by the resident dhobiwallah and the problems of the Emergency had done nothing to stop the regular arrival of mail from the U.K.

Virtually the only breaks from the uncomfortable monotony of patrolling, laying ambushes and guarding the Company base were the occasional very welcome visits to the nearest seaside town which was classified as safe for soldiers to roam without hindrance.

Immediately surrounding the Company base were rubber plantations with many overgrown areas between them. The nearest jungle was only a mile away, close by the local village. Nowhere was the jungle more than three miles away. As Byrne had noticed on his drive to the base, some of the plantations, usually the larger ones, were kept immaculately. Others were almost secondary jungle, where the rubber trees could only be found by following the winding paths trod by the tappers. Some of the larger estates had their own villages near their centres. Others relied for their labour on the men and women that streamed out of the villages on foot and on bicycles early every morning.

As in so much of Malaya, C Company's area provided ideal cover for bandits to lay an ambush for the Army, the Police, a planter or even some

Chinese civilian thought to be an informer. Particularly in the early days, before outlying settlements had been re-sited and surrounded by wire, it was easy for them to approach villages with a much better than evens chance of remaining unseen. As Byrne was told, it was just as easy for C Company to patrol and lay ambushes; the difference being that the bandits could have clear objectives whereas C Company needed information and luck, as well as jungle skills.

The bandits had never attacked and never did attack the Company base. This was not because they might not have been able to fire a few shots at the camp during the night and have got away with it. Bandits usually preferred easier targets and to be in superior numbers, with the jungle at their backs to provide cover for them to quickly fade away.

Byrne quickly became aware of the rivalry between the platoons in the Company. The rivalry was without ill-will. It was as well the competition was friendly, as in a small isolated outpost of the British Army anything other would have made life unpleasant. To an outsider it might have been surprising there was so little friction where soldiers washed, slept, ate and drank Tuborg or Carlsberg beers in conditions of close confinement. Tiger beer, brewed in Singapore, was not on sale. It was rumoured in 8 Platoon, almost certainly without foundation, that this particular brew was the potent product of a chemical process which did not include the use of hops and was guaranteed to turn the normally meekest of soldiers fighting mad.

The 1st Battalion Yorkshire Fusiliers had arrived in Malaya six months earlier and had quickly been moved up-country on active operations. C Company's share of the Battalion's current total of fourteen bandit kills was three. Though other Companies had since killed more, C Company had drawn first blood; 7 Platoon had killed a bandit on only their second patrol. Walking into a small clearing the platoon had unexpectedly come across a small group of resting and unusually careless bandits. In total panic the bandits ran off but one fell as the two leading scouts emptied the magazines of their Owen Guns at the fast-disappearing backs. Surprised or lucky or both, 7 Platoon had opened C Company's account. The Platoon was only mildly disappointed when the dead bandit was identified by the Police as a low-ranking member of the local grandiosely titled Independent Platoon. The .303 rifle that was recovered had belonged to a Special Constable killed the previous year, along with the Assistant Manager of a plantation he was escorting.

The other two successes had been only a week before Byrne's arrival and were the result of a small ambush quickly laid on by members of both 7 and 9 Platoons; an *ad hoc* group of those left behind for various reasons when all three platoons were out on patrol. There was nothing lucky about this operation.

The local Police had received information that late most Wednesdays, a party of bandits went into an as yet unfenced small village five miles away to collect food. Such detailed and firm information seemed too good to be true but could certainly not be ignored by the Company Commander. There was no way of knowing whether the information was inaccurate, a hoax, a trap, genuine or a tip-off supplied by someone with a grudge to work off against bandits whose demands had become excessive or in the hope of a substantial reward. It was after midday when the intelligence was received. There was no time to recall one of the platoons on patrol or to find out whether there were any spare troops available from another Company. Even if time had permitted, the area would have been unfamiliar to them. Sergeant Major Reynolds was put in charge.

As fading light turned the green jungle into a place of deep shadows, mosquitoes began their interminable whining in the ears of C.S.M. Reynolds and his composite section of eight men as they left their truck two miles short of the village. They moved quietly in single file along the track and then made their way into the jungle, giving the village a wide berth to avoid disturbing the dogs. The section moved almost noiselessly, the soldiers picking their way carefully through the thick soft debris on the jungle floor. The moonlight above the trees did not penetrate far below and every now and again there was a louder than normal rustle as a soldier ran his foot into an unseen obstacle. The guilty Fusilier, though he couldn't see it, was uncomfortably conscious of the baleful glance of the C.S.M. levelled in his direction.

There were two tracks, 100 yards apart, leading into the jungle from the village. There was little cover for an ambush between the jungle and the nearest houses. This and the clear moonlight led C.S.M. Reynolds to split his small section into two. He positioned a small ambush party on each track just inside the jungle's edge. His hope was, if bandits did come, they would be caught in the open having passed the waiting riflemen. It was a quiet, warm night. Occasionally a dog barked in the village. There were no other sounds; apparently the villagers went to bed early. The members of 7 and 9 Platoons, who had so unexpectedly been pressed into active service and had been looking forward to a comparatively uneventful few days on guard or escort duty, settled down into firing positions. To a man they wished they were back in camp, either drinking a cold beer in the canteen or playing pontoon in off-duty moments in the guard tent. They were no strangers to fruitless ambushes laid on by enthusiastic officers.

Not one of them really expected much more than a boring and mosquito-ridden night.

Unexpectedly, shortly after 9.30 p.m., the enemy arrived. Simultaneously the Fusiliers' hearts beat faster and a cold empty feeling gripped their stomachs. Six bandits, four carrying rifles and two clutching Sten guns, warily came down the track in single file. They looked apprehensively from side to side, almost as if expecting trouble. The leading two were almost opposite the undergrowth in which Reynolds and three of his men lay concealed before they were spotted, so carefully had they approached. It was as if the two leading bandits' sixth sense told them there was imminent danger but there was little chance that they could have seen the by now sweating Fusiliers. The leading bandit, now opposite the ambush position and only five yards away, stopped and exchanged urgent words with the man behind him. They both turned round, loudly whispered to the remaining four and began to retrace their steps. There was no point in waiting and hoping for a bigger target. Reynolds fired, immediately followed by the rest. The four men could hardly miss at such close range. The stillness of the night was shattered by a cacophony of gunfire. The two Chinese in front of the position were sprayed with bullets from two Sten guns and as many as could be fired in a few seconds by the two riflemen, who worked the bolts of their weapons as fast as their excitement allowed. The two bandits fell instantly, hit, it turned out later, by eleven bullets between them. One of the remaining four bandits fired one shot from his rifle which swished harmlessly into the leaves above, as he turned panic-stricken with the others and rapidly disappeared from sight into the trees on either side of the track – pursued by optimistic shots from C.S.M. Reynolds and his triumphant section. They stopped firing. The sinking feeling in their stomachs slowly being replaced by one of elation. C Company had scored. They could already hear the congratulations of their Company Commander and somewhat envious Platoon Commanders and had begun to rehearse the stories they would be able to tell.

Other than to check the area to see if there were any signs of other bandits having been wounded, there was little else to do. There was no point in trying to find fleeing bandits at night in the jungle. The Company Commander would decide in the morning if it was worth mounting a follow-up operation. They searched the bodies. One rifle and a Sten gun were recovered along with two small Japanese hand grenades, relics of the recent occupation.

C.S.M. Reynolds called in the other ambush section and the signaller slung his aerial into the trees and tried to contact Company H.Q. The understandable eagerness of the Sergeant Major and his men to report their success was only rivalled by the poorness of the communications that night. Repeated tuning and netting calls only resulted in fragmented and unintelligible conversations. Eventually despairing of getting through and unwilling to wait about until morning, when atmospheric conditions usually improved. C.S.M. Reynolds sent a Corporal and a small party on a long trek to the nearest planter's house to telephone for transport.

It was approaching dawn before the two bullet-ridden bodies were brought back to camp, already wreathed in that unpleasant, rich sickly smell of flesh beginning to decay. To those who hadn't seen a bandit, dead or alive, before, the two looked small and insignificant; no different from the hundreds of Chinese seen every day going about their lawful business. The only evidence of their trade was the two weapons and one red-starred khaki hat. There was a minor but friendly dispute on its disposal. All the members of the success-ful ambush naturally claimed to have been the first to have shot the bandit that had sported this much-valued headgear. As rank had no privileges in such matters, a mini-raffle decided who should keep this souvenir.

During the days that followed C.S.M. Reynold's successful ambush, there was a general feeling of self-satisfaction in C Company. However, 8 Platoon became increasingly conscious that they had not contributed to the Company's small list of successes. Not one shot had been fired in anger by them or at them. Though they had assiduously patrolled and laid ambushes, not one bandit had they seen. They had not seen even traces of their elusive quarry. Contrary to what anxious mothers and fathers may have thought back home, this was often the experience of many platoons for month after month. Patience was a necessity but it was a difficult lesson for young and easily bored soldiers to learn. Though with some-thing of an understandable feeling that they had been somewhat left out of things, the morale of 8 Platoon remained satisfactorily high. Byrne found this inherent cheerfulness comforting. He often wondered, remembering the lessons on leadership taught at Eaton Hall, who was leading who in keeping up their collective spirits. Particularly cheerful and not surpris-ingly so, was Second Lieutenant Atkins, 8 Platoon Commander. Atkins was shortly to hand the Platoon over to Byrne and return home having completed his two years National Service. Though confessing genuine disappointment at the lack of success in the previous months, Atkins attributed this entirely to bad luck. Given just half the chances of the other platoons, he forcefully maintained to his fellow Platoon Commanders, 8 Platoon would have done twice as well. An opinion, needless to say, shared by the members of that Platoon.

The day of Byrne's jungle baptism arrived. The patrol got off to a 4.00 a.m. start. Four Dodge open flat trucks on dipped headlights moved smoothly out of camp and turned left on to the main road, keeping engine noise down to the minimum. 'No point in advertising to the locals,' said Atkins over his shoulder to Byrne. Byrne found the early morning cool breeze, caused by the truck's movement, very refreshing. He examined his well-cleaned and carefully-oiled W.W.II M1 carbine for the umpteenth time. It was a light weapon, considered suitable for Platoon Commanders. At Eaton Hall it had been stressed more than once that an Officer was there to direct the fire of his men and not to act as a rifleman. Atkins had told him the carbine wasn't much use for stopping bandits in their tracks, unless they were hit in a vital place. The bullets tended to 'fight clean' and leave the bandit still running. It certainly felt insubstantial compared with the sturdy .303 Byrne had been used to in his basic training. The members of the Platoon carried the weapons they preferred. The Company possessed a variety of weapons. The two leading scouts, Brockley and Hird, carried angular Owen guns of Australian origin. Private Rice, Atkins' batman whom Byrne was shortly to inherit, carried a Sten gun with a handsome polished wooden stock, of which he was inordinately proud. Spratt, a big man, carried a Bren gun, slung from his shoulders with the aid of a sling. The rest of the Platoon carried either Sten guns or the Mark V .303 Lee Enfield. The latter had a flash eliminator and was a shorter barrelled version of the standard and longer Mk 1V version of W.W.II fame. The decreased length of the Mk V made it less of an encumbrance in the jungle and more suitable for use at close-quarters. It was a popular weapon. No-one was in any doubt, if a bandit was knocked over by a .303 bullet, even in the arm, he was likely to stay down for some time. Burton, the tallest and strongest of the platoon, predictably called 'Shorty', carried the heavy wireless set which rested in a harness on his back. Though he, too, carried a rifle, when on longer patrols his rations were distributed among the other members of the Platoon. Byrne was never to know this gentle giant complain of his burden, no matter how hot the day or how many miles had to be covered.

The trucks stopped briefly where a timber wagon track led off the road into the jungle. The Platoon quickly and quietly debussed and took up positions of all-round defence. It was half-light and a time when the jungle looked at its least inviting. The trucks returned to camp, the small escort taking markedly more interest in the jungle edges now their passengers had gone.

The two leading scouts set off at a slow pace, one slightly ahead of the other, on either side of the track. Their index fingers were along the trigger guards as they looked for anything unusual in the dark recesses of the jungle fringe. Atkins let them get about twenty yards ahead and then set off himself, motioning Byrne to take up station behind him. A rifleman, then Spratt with his Bren gun followed, with the Platoon Sergeant, Sergeant Lennox, not far behind. Leaving the Platoon Commander to attend to matters tactical, Sergeant Lennox occasionally glanced back to ensure everyone was alert and the spacing between the members of the Platoon was to his satisfaction. Byrne did his best to look experienced and professional. At least his brand-new green jungle boots, tightly laced up his shin, were getting muddy for the first time. The day started to lighten and get warmer. Like the rest of the Platoon, dark patches of sweat started to appear on Byrne's shirt.

Nobody actually walked in the middle of the track. Not only because it was not a sensible tactical thing to do – the centre was farthest away from the nearest cover – but because the track was mostly a deep stagnant river of bright light-brown mud, churned up by heavily laden lorries. Though not a military thought, Byrne could not help noticing the pleasing colour scheme created by the bright brown mud, the green trees and the blue sky overhead. Though woodcutters started work early, they would not be ahead of the Platoon. The curfew would have seen to that. Byrne walked on with his carbine at the ready, peering carefully between the trees into the undergrowth on his side of the track, hoping the man behind him was keeping an equally close watch on the other. This was the first time he had entered the jungle. He was quick to realise that if there had been bandits lying in wait a few yards away, they only had to have grasped the basic rudiments of camouflage for him not to see them. The first he would know of their presence, he thought, would be shots fired at him from a range at which they could not possibly miss. It gave him an uncomfortable feeling. However, the rest of the Platoon didn't appear to share his concern, at least they showed no outward signs. He comforted himself that it would be a stroke of the worst possible luck that of all the jungle tracks in Malaya, this one had been selected by the bandits for a speculative ambush that morning.

One of Second Lieutenant Atkins's instructions for the day was to introduce Byrne to the art of patrolling. In slow time, the Company Commander had said, observing all the rules and preferably with no unnecessary excitement – though realising that tranquillity could never be guaranteed. By now 8 Platoon was well over a mile into the jungle. There were only a few dry patches on their shirts, even though up till then exertion had been modest.

From a long way behind they heard the faint noise of lorries grinding away in low gear. It slowly grew louder. Atkins raised his arm and swept it from side to side. The Platoon quietly and swiftly moved a few yards into the jungle, faced the track and sank into firing positions. Byrne followed suit. The loud heavy groaning of labouring engines grew ever louder. Two dilapidated timber lorries finally appeared from round the bend. They lurched from side to side as every few yards the wheels sank into deeper potholes, pushing out waves of shiny mud. A dozen or so Chinese woodcutters clung precariously to the superstructures. Atkins waited till the first lorry was nearly opposite him and both were in the middle of the Platoon's position. He stepped out into the track and raised his hand in the manner of a traffic policeman. Taking their cue, the rest of the platoon stepped forward with their weapons at the ready. Byrne saw the expressions of the Chinese turn from horror to relief. Whether this was because they were genuinely pleased to see British soldiers rather than the local bandits, who might have relieved them of any money and food they had with them, was impossible to say. Atkins ordered a search of the vehicles and their passengers. This did not take long as there were few hiding places in the skeletal lorries or the skimpy clothing of the wood-cutters. On more than one occasion, Atkins said, he had turned labourers over to the Police who had been caught carrying rice and tins of food in sufficient quantities to create serious doubts as to its eventual destination. This time there were no grounds for suspicion. The woodcutters' papers were in order and there were no abnormal amounts of food to be found. Atkins waved them about their business and the lorries lurched off on their swishy, muddy way with a noisy crashing of gears. The labourers, still tenaciously clinging to whatever handhold they could find, waved a cheerful farewell.

The Platoon followed in the shiny wake of the lorries for half a mile. They came to a fork in the track. It was obvious the lorries had swung right. 'Not a lot of point in going up there,' said Atkins, 'by now there'll be no bandits for miles in any direction, even if there were any around to start with', cynically referring to the virtual certainty of at least one of the woodcutters deliberately or inadvertently telling any bandit he might come across of the close proximity of the security forces. Atkins led the Platoon up the left fork. After another two miles it petered out in a large clearing with here and there massive piles of felled trees. A brief consul-tation between Atkins and Sergeant Lennox resulted in the welcome and hoped-for decision that it was time to 'take five'. Sentries were posted, tommy cookers, water bottles and mess tins were quickly produced and the British soldier settled happily into the Army's traditional ritual of making tea and with less enthusiasm, to eat the unimaginative cheese sandwiches provided by the Company cooks.

The quiet of the break was interrupted. 'They've been here at some time, Sir,' said Sergeant Lennox, examining a handful of damp and grubby sheets of paper one of the sentries had found behind a large log. A further search of the area revealed several more of the same. From their dilapidated condition they had clearly been there for many days. The papers were crudely duplicated pamphlets, printed in purple and red, depicting what was meant to be a very smart bandit in a heroic warlike pose holding a tommy gun, a red star prominent on his baggy cap. Alongside this imposing figure was shown a diminutive and distinctly unheroic-looking British soldier with a careworn and apprehensive appearance. He unconvincingly clutched a rifle, looked very homesick and in short was the very antithesis of the noble member of the Malayan Races Liberation Army shown alongside.

The poorly handwritten caption was to the effect that down-trodden British soldiers were being exploited by their imperialistic and rich officers who had obtained their wealth by grinding the faces of the working classes. The only logical and proper revolutionary solution to this intolerable situation, the pamphlet explained, was for the soldiers to leave their officers immediately and to seek out the forces of liberation. On meeting their deliverers they should hand over their rifles and join in the struggle for freedom. The reaction of the Platoon was one of hilarity. A spontaneous and lively discussion ensued. There was speculation as to which member of the Platoon most closely resembled the miserable specimen of an oppressed British soldier depicted on the pamphlet. Rice, Atkins's batman, appeared to be the popular choice as an obvious servant of the ruling class. Several not very veiled hints were dropped that, if either of the two Officers were thinking of giving away some spare dollars from their vast family fortunes, there were members of 8 Platoon only too willing to help them out. Second Lieutenant Atkins, the son of an impecunious and very junior local government officer, was quick to point out that he was well aware the bank balances of some of them were much bigger than his own and it was only King's Regulations that had stopped him asking for a loan. Putting two copies of the pamphlet into his pocket for the attention of the Battalion Intelligence Officer, Atkins distributed the remainder among the Platoon to add to their collections of souvenirs. Byrne and Atkins both wondered what purpose the bandits had in producing such crude propaganda. Presumably they must have thought it might have some marginal effect on morale, surely they could not believe for one moment that it might encourage desertions or cause a mutiny? As Atkins remarked, if they believed that they would believe anything. It only confirmed his long-held view that the Communist fanatic lived in a world of his own, not only misjudging the determination of his enemy but, far more importantly, grossly overestimating the desire of the population to embrace the principles of Marx and Lenin. It was a pity the bandits hadn't been watching the reactions of his Platoon. There again, fanatics were not noted for a sense of humour.

Tea finished and weapons checked, the Platoon struck off straight into the jungle on a direct five-mile trek to the pre-arranged rendezvous with the transport. Atkins explained and Byrne had already guessed, thinking back to what he had been taught, that taking the same patrol route out as in could be asking for trouble; particularly as the route in had already been well-publicised to the local Chinese. Such an obvious mistake, combined with a speculative and hastily laid bandit ambush, could well result in unnecessary casualties with only a fleeting chance of inflicting any in return.

The remaining hours of the patrol were uneventful. Primary jungle was much more passable than Byrne had been led to imagine from those wartime film epics where soldiers cursed, sweated and slashed slow paths through dense tangles of branches and vines, making enough noise to alert the enemy for miles around. In some places he could even imagine, if it were not for the humidity and the immense size of the trees, that he was in an English forest. The last few hundred yards to the road were different. Having been cleared at one time in the past, the resulting secondary growth was a mass of dense vegetation and thorns, through which there was no option other than to force a way. Scratched, hot and slightly out of breath, Byrne rather more than the rest, 8 Platoon waited by the roadside for the trucks to take them back to camp for a welcome wash, beer and sleep.

Chapter 5

Lessons Learnt

'Life begins at nineteen,' reflected Second Lieutenant Andrew Byrne as he relaxed in a comfortable chair on the small verandah of the wooden building that was C Company's Officers' Mess. In the cool of a tropical evening, with a glass of gin topped up with lime juice and ice in one hand, puffing on a pipe he had bought in the hope that it made him appear older and more mature, he felt at peace with the world.

Seven weeks had passed since he had arrived at C Company in his newly-made and freshly-starched shorts and shirt, long grey socks, shining brown boots and puttees; the last-mentioned neatly wrapped, in the approved fashion, round the otherwise untidy boundary between the top of his boots and socks. After two more patrols under the tutelage of Atkins, now some weeks departed after an uproarious and beery platoon party, 8 Platoon belonged to him. He already felt an intense pride in the Platoon. A pride of possession that he had so clearly seen in Atkins. Byrne had absolutely no doubts in his mind that he commanded the finest soldiers in C Company, which naturally meant the best in Malaya.

The patrols he had been ordered to carry out since he had taken over the Platoon had been even less eventful than the first. Elsewhere, however, during the last seven weeks, there had been successes and the Battalion had added three more bandits to the score. B Company had killed two and A Company one. The two had been killed after B Company had been passed information about bandits being regularly seen on a distant rubber estate near a small group of rubber tappers' huts. After three patient days in a well-laid ambush, two had been caught emerging from the jungle on a food-hunting expedition. The other success was not the result of planning. A platoon from A Company was being driven back to base and came across a group of bandits actually preparing an ambush position by the road, almost certainly intended for the local planter and his escort who frequently used that route. By the time the frenetic exchange of fire had died down and the eight panic-stricken bandits had scattered, the score was A Company 1, Bandits 0. Though six bullet holes in an A Company truck subsequently had to be hammered out by the Company's vehicle mechanic.

For several weeks, all three platoons in C Company had been out on a succession of patrols and occasional ambushes with few nights of relaxation in camp. Information on the activities of the bandits was in short supply. However, the growing impression in 8 Platoon that there were no bandits in the area had been abruptly corrected by the murder of a male Chinese, in front of his family, near a small village on the edge of the Company's area. It had been a brutal and cowardly shooting. Almost certainly, the local Police Inspector had said, because the unfortunate man had not been sufficiently co-operative in providing food or was suspected of supplying information to the Security Forces.

The following day, returning from Battalion Headquarters after an intelligence briefing, the Company Commander assured his three subalterns that the powers that be were quite convinced there were plenty of bandits in the Company's area. The Commanding Officer had been kind enough to venture the opinion that it had only been C Company's intensive patrolling that had caused the bandits to keep their heads down and to confine their terrorist activities to the shooting of a defenceless civilian. However, though the bandits were being cautious, they wouldn't and couldn't remain inactive for ever. They were still collecting food themselves or picking it up from pre-arranged dumps but the rumour in the kampongs was that the supply was not proving enough. The Battalion Intelligence Officer was convinced they would eventually be forced to take some risks, however small. Sooner or later the bandits would want to boost their self-confidence and try to add to their credibility as a force to be reckoned with. The local population could not be allowed to believe normality had returned to at least one State in Malaya. They desperately needed a success, even a minor one, against the Police or the Army. They might even decide a few shots fired from a sufficiently long distance at a planter's bungalow would be considered a sufficiently heroic action. It was only a question of information, keeping up the pressure and as always, a modicum of luck, said the Company Commander. There would be a contact with the bandits, the only unknown factor was when. Though inwardly hoping they would do well when the time came, that moment couldn't come too soon for 8 Platoon.

Not that 8 Platoon was downhearted, far from it. The sheer hard work of patrolling, day after day, left little time to be sorry for oneself for very long. Though when lying in ambush, sweating, trying to keep awake, cursing the unwanted mosquitoes and watching a track down which nothing came, often caused the most dedicated 8 Platoon conscript to visualise places he would much rather be.

By now Byrne was getting to know the Platoon much better. Sergeant Lennox, the professional soldier had, if anything, even more regard for his Platoon of National Servicemen than Byrne himself. Though a Scot serving in a Yorkshire Regiment of Fusiliers, there was no mistaking his pride in his Regiment in general and in 8 Platoon, C Company, of the 1st Battalion in particular. He made no secret of his craving for a success. It was he who enthusiastically welcomed each operation, assiduously checking weapons and ammunition and making sure that only the favourite and most useful tins of food were carried in the Platoon's packs. Tins of cheese and jam were discarded for stewed steak and vegetables. Extra tea, milk and sugar were essential. Sergeant Lennox was altogether a tower of strength. Byrne had quickly grown to value his wise advice and support, his stoicism when things went wrong and his tolerance of his own errors of judgement when he first took over the Platoon.

Private 'Shorty' Burton, the wireless operator, was an inveterate cigarette smoker. It was he who insisted on the non-smoking members of the Platoon drawing their free weekly-issued tin of fifty full-size Woodbines. Circulating afterwards, he would gratefully collect tins, free of charge, from his closest friends and haggle over the price with those less friendly and short of funds. Every evening when on operations, it was his personal task to contact the Company base to radio a situation report. He rarely failed to get through, even though atmospheric conditions often presented difficulties. These technical problems were of only passing interest to the rest of the Platoon who inevitably would be more engrossed in the progress of the evening meal. The exception was if Burton was trying to signal a rendezvous and a time for transport to pick them up the following day. If he failed to make contact, in spite of considerable encouragement, his popularity took a turn for the worse and there were fewer promises of free cigarettes in the future.

Privates Brockley and Hird, the leading scouts, were as inseparable in camp as they were in the jungle. Though Middlesbrough dockers in civilian life, they thought of themselves as professional soldiers. National Service pay, though, they occasionally complained, didn't even start to compare with that in civilian life. After a few weeks, Byrne decided that it would only be fair to give other members of the Platoon a turn as leading scouts. After all, he reasoned, he had been taught that the more arduous or dangerous duties should be shared. The decision was a mistake. Even though he explained the impeccable logic of the change, it was a much disgruntled Brockley and Hird who took up unaccustomed places back in the middle of the Platoon on the next patrol. One day of hurt looks and sulking was more than enough for Byrne. Their personal pride had been severely dented and their prowess called into question. The next day found them once again leading the Platoon, swinging their Owen guns slowly from side to side, keeping watchful eyes on the surrounding jungle.

Private Spratt, the Bren Gunner, aspired to be a successful professional boxer. His flattish nose testified to many an amateur bout. A keep-fit fanatic, he would occasionally manage to persuade other members of the Company to spar with him. Byrne had learnt his lesson and politely refused invitations to take part. He was thankful that his own strictly limited prowess in the noble art had not reached Spratt's ears.

Not all the characters were in 8 Platoon. The Company was packed with them. One of the most notorious was Private Gingell, the water-truck driver. When conscripts had been assigned to their various trades, someone with a warped sense of humour, or bereft of skills in selection, had decided that Gingell was to be a driver. He was an extremely enthusiastic but totally incompetent member of the Mechanical Transportation Section. Vehicles and Gingell did not mix. How he had passed his driving test was a frequent matter for speculation. His ambition in life was to be assigned away from his unglamorous and solid water truck to a Dodge flat fifteen cwt. so he could help move the platoons about or collect stores. Better still, perhaps Mr. Byrne would use his influence to let him drive a Land-Rover or the Humber Scout Car? In fact, he was prepared to drive anything as long as it wasn't the water truck. As one of the longer serving drivers, he thought his status was affronted and his skills undervalued. The Corporal in charge of the Company's transport also had an ambition. This was quite simply not to let Gingell anywhere near another vehicle and if possible, get him moved out of the section altogether. He had no luck at all in trying to persuade the Company Commander that Gingell would make a first-class rifleman in one of the platoons. The Signals and Cook Sergeants were decidedly unimpressed when Gingell was offered on a free transfer. The M.T. Corporal had, however, in desperation, forbidden Gingell to drive any other vehicle than the water truck under threat of punishments too horrible even to contemplate. Between trips he was employed on the job where it was considered he would do the least harm, washing down the Company's vehicles. Each morning, it was a familiar sight to see Private Gingell drive the water truck out of camp, with the escort vehicle being driven warily a much longer distance behind than was normal, narrowly missing the camp posts, to the excruciating sound of a badly mistreated gear box.

The Company Commander had told Byrne when he first arrived that this was a Platoon Commander's war. At times, it was even the Section Commander who had to take the quick decision that could make the difference between success and failure. Nothing had happened in the first few weeks to lead Byrne to disagree with this assessment. Even though C Company's Platoons were always below strength and never had more than twenty-five men in each, there were rarely operational reasons for a patrol stronger than a platoon. Though a Company could conceivably establish itself in the jungle, it would be from that base that platoon or section patrols would fan out to search. Very large numbers of bandits were rarely found in camps or on the move in the Battalion's area. Bigger bandit groups occasionally did come together for a large set-piece ambush to attack a Police Station or a planter's bungalow. Such more daring and spectacular incidents were rare. Other than on their own terms, with numbers very much on their side, the bandits usually avoided contact with the Security Forces. Personal bravery and imaginative military tactics did not bulk large in the bandits' tactical repertoire.

In recent months there had only been one large scale operation. The Battalion, including C Company, had played a prominent, if ineffectual, part. Planned by the Brigade Commander, who had a sense of humour, OPERATION M.R.L.A. stood for Massacre Reds with Lethal Ambushes. The grandiose plan was for no less than two battalions, in as straight a line as it was possible to achieve, to work their way slowly south through about thirty miles of jungle. The aim was to drive a bandit Independent Platoon, believed to be in a particular green patch on the map, ahead of them. The bandits, presumably in an advanced state of nervous anxiety verging on panic, were then expected to walk into the killing grounds of several ambushes, placed on likely tracks. These multiple ambushes were provided by A, C and D Companies of the 1st Battalion Yorkshire Fusiliers. Added punch was to be added to OPERATION M.R.L.A. by a Royal Artillery Regiment of 25-pounders and several air strikes, which between them would provide an intermittent creeping barrage in front of the advancing troops and hopefully help speed the bandits to their inevitable doom. The practical difficulties seemed insuperable to the average Private

Soldier but the concept looked splendid when marked on a map with variously coloured chinagraph pencils.

OPERATION M.R.L.A. was not a success. If there had been a bandit Independent Platoon in the area, its fleeing members didn't pass within sight of C Company or anyone else for that matter. The Ghurkhas, jungle fighters *par excellence*, who provided one of the two battalions doing the job of beaters, found their ability to move through the jungle in deadly silence put to the test by patches of jungle well and truly churned up by shells and bombs.

8 Platoon's contribution to the operation was placing ambushes of six men each on two tracks, day and night, for three days. The ambush positions were 400 yards apart on tracks leading into the jungle from a small village. If nothing else, it was excellent training. The Platoon became adept at changing over the ambushers at four-hour intervals. In an orderly sequence, the riflemen would quietly slide back into the undergrowth to be replaced by others; their faces freshly blackened and green face veils helping to break up what little silhouette they presented. The mosquitoes kept them company for most of the three days. There was no excitement. One ambush was more popular than the other in that in the far distance, the local Chinese ladies could be seen performing their morning ablutions in a nearby stream. It was obvious the presence of British soldiers had not been detected as the ladies, some extremely attractive, happily chattered and splashed away in various stages of undress. To the chagrin of 8 Platoon, the distance to the stream was just too far, even for the keenest-sighted, for more than general details to be seen, though more than near enough to be tantalising. Not surprisingly, Byrne found it necessary to issue stern reminders from time to time on the real purpose of the British Army in Malaya; which was not the one that crossed the minds of the soldiers lying in the undergrowth watching the aquatic gambols of Chinese maidens.

The other ambush position was less popular. It was more than a fraction too near where pigs were kept. A fact that was only too obvious when the occasional breeze blew from the wrong direction. The smell was foul. No-one was unhappy when instructions to return to base was received over the radio. OPERATION M.R.L.A. had proved once again it was not often a General's war.

From the example of the rest of the Platoon, Byrne had learnt the art of moving through the jungle silently. This meant avoiding obstacles where possible, including evading any more obvious awkward features that could be seen in the distance, as well as those of a lesser nature close to.

Simply plodding in a straight line, regardless of what might lie ahead, was obviously not intelligent. Detours were required; short detours round occasional patches of particularly unpleasant or dense vegetation and longer ones around a more major obstacle such as a steep-sided ravine. The erratic courses Byrne had to steer for hours on end forced him to become an expert with map and compass and estimating distance.

In the more remote parts of the jungle, maps were not so much inaccurate, as frequently lacking in important detail. Detail mattered to the soldiers of 8 Platoon when every yard was covered on foot, particularly at the beginning of a long patrol when packs were heavy. Major features, particularly the higher hills, could normally be relied upon to help pinpoint the Platoon's location by a judicious use of back-bearings. That is, when they could be seen sufficiently clearly through the greenery above to be identified with certainty. Of less help were the smaller hills and streams which frequently looked much alike. For many miles during a patrol it was often impossible to find a feature which positively related to a set of contour lines on the map. This, together with frequent detours, meant that Byrne had two ever-present concerns in navigating. He had to ensure he kept the Platoon on the correct bearing as far as was practical. At the same time he had to make allowances for the distances they had moved to left or right and make a compensating change to their direction when the opportunity offered. This was a task that Sergeant Lennox was more than happy to leave to his Platoon Commander. He saw his own duty as one of making sure the Platoon stayed alert at all times, didn't bunch up and kept quiet.

For many patrols, the fact that the Platoon occasionally might stray a little off course didn't matter overmuch. A contact with bandits or, more likely, traces of their presence, could as well be in one map square as in the next. On other occasions it was very important, as the Company Commander had pointed out; for example, if the object of the patrol was to lay an undetected ambush in a specific place. In order to get there, an unseen long approach march through the jungle might be necessary, avoiding houses, rubber estates and other places of work. Accurate navigation was required if there was to be any hope of success. It was equally important, in the eyes of the Platoon, towards the end of a patrol lasting many days, that the map reference where the transport was expected was not missed by much. The finish of a patrol was preferably not to be extended by an extra hike of several hot and humid miles. Byrne knew that an inexpert or piece of careless navigation on his part could result in the loss of several points on the popularity scale. As the weeks passed, he found that with continuing practice and growing experience, a directional sixth sense developed. This meant he did not have to glance surreptitiously at his map and check his compass bearing every few hundred yards, so avoiding any suspicions in the minds of the Platoon that he was lost.

There was a brief but pleasant interlude when a Platoon of Ghurkhas visited the Company. A neighbouring Ghurkha Company was due to take over some of the Company's area in the south and this required the formality of a briefing by C Company Commander and a reconnaissance. This was the first time Byrne had seen these cheerful, small brown soldiers at close quarters. He had heard many times from his Mother that his Grandfather had held them in high regard. He also had been a Yorkshire Fusilier and had served for many years in India before the turn of the century. In the years before his death in W.W.I he had often mentioned his liking and respect for the loyal and courageous soldiers from Nepal. Byrne spent many happy hours touring the countryside with their Platoon Commander and a Ghurkha escort. Their alertness and keenness set a standard Byrne determined he and his Platoon would emulate. He was comforted that they were on the same side as C Company. They had a formidable reputation. Rumour had it, not surprisingly, that of the Security Forces, the Ghurkhas were feared by the bandits most of all. Following their visit there was a minor upsurge in the buying of the chromium-plated kukris advertised for sale by the Regimental Shop.

The tactics adopted by C Company to combat terrorism were clear-cut and little different from those of the other Companies. Obviously one was to seek out the bandits wherever they could be found. They could be in their camps, on the move singly or in pairs as couriers, in groups going to or coming from an operation or escorting a high-ranking communist on a tour of visits.

The other major tactic was to reduce the bandits' supply of information and especially food, from the Min Yuen. The Min Yuen was the communists' non-uniformed civilian organisation whose members, to all outward appearances, were indistinguishable from the rest of the civilian population. The logic for this latter tactic was straightforward. The more difficult it was for the bandits to get food, the more risks they would have to take to get it and the less time they would have to take the offensive against the planters, the Police and the rest of the Security Forces. The more risks they took, arising from a combination of bandit frustration and hunger, the more likely it was that they would make that final and fatal mistake. These tactics appeared to work, not only with C Company but in the rest of the Battalion's operational area. So well did they work that in the later stages of the Emergency, starving and ill-clad bandits surrendered in increasing numbers. Assisted by the fencing off and occasional relocation of villages, the formation of a Home Guard, stringent searches at the gates and active patrolling and ambushing, bandits more frequently (in twos and threes) started to venture out of the jungle to bully petrified rubber tappers with threats into bringing them food. The more dedicated Min Yuen members started to take chances they would not previously have even contemplated. The Battalions's score of kills rose slowly and steadily every month.

Success often depended on getting a patrol into the jungle quietly and without being seen. This could prove difficult. Though there was little doubt virtually all the Malays and the vast majority of Chinese did not want to have anything to do with the bandits, not much imagination was required to believe that the man driving his water buffaloes down the road or the ostensibly friendly tapper loping along with his latex container on his back, or an alert woodcutter, just might spread the news that troops were in the area – resulting in the bandits lying low or moving out.

Byrne had tried and would try many devices to move 8 Platoon into the area in secret. Some may have been original, others were certainly not so. Jumping off the back of a moving truck during the night on some unfrequented road was often practised, as was ostentatiously setting off down the road in one direction and then doubling back down a convenient track. Byrne thought up a variation on the truck ploy. He borrowed two low-sided civilian lorries from a local contractor and used them to take the Platoon to the dropping-off point on their next patrol. This particular initiative was not popular with 8 Platoon. The borrowed vehicles had not been cleaned out and there was little doubt in the soldiers' minds, as they lay on the floor, what the previous cargo had been.

In his first two months, Byrne believed he had begun to appreciate some of the finer points about leading a platoon. Like so many other things in life, the more he learnt, the greater his realisation was of how much more there was to understand and to practise. The principles were the same as he had been taught at Eaton Hall. Their application in the jungle was another matter.

To his mild surprise, man-management had not been a problem. He found himself gaining increasing confidence from the mere presence of the handful of cheerful National Service Yorkshire Fusiliers he felt himself privileged to lead. If the members of 8 Platoon were dissatisfied with their lot, it rarely showed. They deserved a success, he decided, and made his way to the paraffin-powered refrigerator for another glass of gin, lime juice and ice.

Chapter 6

Snakes Alive

The jungle was neutral, Byrne decided. Other things being equal, it favoured or hindered both sides of the conflict in equal part. But other things were not always equal. On the whole, as might be expected, it was kinder to the ambusher than the ambushed and to the pursued rather than the pursuer. The bandits' principal military tactic was a well-laid ambush, whenever they were not busy avoiding the patrols of the Security Forces. Unlike the Army's ambushes, the bandits preferred to spread their men along an embankment overlooking a minor estate road and occasionally a major trunk road, down which they had reason to expect a lightly guarded planter's vehicle or a small military or police convoy – with the jungle at their backs for a swift retreat.

As C Company did not expect to find bandits marching down the road very often, their ambushes tended to be in the jungle or its edge. In such close country there was rarely time to get off more than a handful of shots before the intended victims vanished among the trees with hopefully one or two dead left behind. The jungle did favour those who wanted to avoid contact with the enemy and made life correspondingly more difficult for those seeking it. The problem was that the Army and the Police Jungle Squads were in the latter category. As it was neither an exciting nor practical proposition just to sit hopefully in camp and patiently wait for information, which might never come, on which to act, 8 Platoon came in for their fair share of seemingly aimless days of 'jungle-bashing'. Even though, to the ordinary soldier, the main purpose of these expeditions might have been to fill out the Company's evening Situation Report to Battalion H.Q., the endless patrolling served to remind the bandits and civilian population alike that the Government was in charge.

Diversions, other than the irritating attention of mosquitoes, abounded in this part of the tropics. There were waist-deep swamps to wade through. Leeches sometimes insinuated themselves under the jungle-greens and had to be displaced using a lighted match or cigarette end. Prickly heat rashes, when skin peeled off in painfully suppurating sheets, appeared in the most sensitive parts of the body – the remedy for which was the application of a purplish iodine-based solution which temporarily caused excruciating agony to the sufferer. There was an unpleasant condition known to the soldiers as 'foot-rot', which caused feet to look as if they had had the attention of tiny burrowing creatures.

On the credit side, though the rain was often torrential, it was never really cold, even at night. Drying-out was only a matter of time. Even after crossing a chest-high river, it did not take many miles of walking in the heat for the last drop of moisture to disappear. There were glorious small and large waterfalls to see with welcome cool and sparkling water. Occasionally small sandy beaches were alongside clear green-fringed streams.

Compared with the greater denseness and enervating, still heat of lower-lying jungle, on the upper slopes the trees thinned out and refreshing breezes could sometimes be found. From a vantage point, there were vistas of mile after mile of rolling gloriously green jungle and blue sky. Occasionally, on deeper patrols, 8 Platoon would fleetingly come across the aborigines. Called, somewhat superciliously, Sakai by the Malays, they were the friendly and shy original inhabitants of the Malay Peninsula.

After his first few patrols, Byrne rarely thought much about the jungle wildlife. Neither did the rest of the Platoon. Though their expectancy was initially high, perhaps the result of watching too many Tarzan films, they saw little in the way of animal or reptile life and interest faded. No doubt the permanent inhabitants of the jungle took good care to keep out of their way. Distant sightings of animal life were rare and closer contacts even more so. Once, in the beam of the searchlight when on pilot-train duty, on a long stretch of line, they had seen elephants crossing the track far ahead. The first and last time 8 Platoon would see them.

One night the Platoon had settled into their bashas for as sound a night's sleep as was possible given the interminable whining of mosquitoes. A basha was a one-man ridge tent, easily made from a poncho. A wise man carried two pieces of mosquito netting to drape across the open ends. This at least kept the whirring pests from closer and more irritating contact.

Private Rice, Byrne's batman, was one of the three sentries. It was unlikely bandits would ever attack a platoon base in the middle of the jungle at night, even if they knew it was there. However, Sergeant Lennox was not a regular soldier for nothing and took no chances. He took pride in ensuring there was always a sentry duty roster. Everyone took their turn on 'stag' and in consultation with Byrne, he placed the sentries carefully to cover any possible lines of enemy approach. A 'Stand-to' at both dusk and dawn was also faithfully observed by 8 Platoon, even though this routine was probably more applicable to conventional warfare against a much less elusive opponent.

It was the small hours of the morning when Private Rice tugged at Byrne's foot and requested permission to shoot the tiger. As might be imagined, this was not an enquiry that Byrne had previously encountered. In this respect he was almost certainly not unique among all the Platoon Commanders in Malaya, both before and since. Byrne was immediately wide-awake. Even allowing for Rice's bubbling enthusiasm and occasional youthful eagerness to shoot things, he realised something must have caused this unusual petition. Quietly, Rice led his Platoon Commander the few yards to his sentry position. Some ten yards away was a large shape which blended almost totally into the general blackness beyond. In the dark mass were two glowing eyes. It could only be a tiger. Byrne's first inner reaction was one of amazement at Rice's initial restraint in not shooting when he first saw the animal. Secondly, he was surprised at the obliging nature of the rimau, the Malay name for tiger, to have stayed where it was in order to be observed at such close quarters, or even shot at.

While Byrne was still assessing, with little success, how to deal with the unusual tactical situation in which he had been placed, Rice eased the bolt of his Sten gun back and down from the safety into the cocked position. He suggested, in a loud whisper, that he should open fire and shoot the intruder. Byrne made his first decision and put aside all thoughts of a possible tiger-skin rug. Shots in the jungle, particularly in the relative still of the night, would be heard for miles. If that happened, the patrol might just as well return to base the following morning. Further, even though the animal was very close, Rice might still miss, in view of his strictly limited experience of night-firing at tigers. On the other hand, the tiger might only be wounded. That would be an act of cruelty. It might attack, with unpredictable results, almost certainly to the general discomfiture of the members of 8 Platoon who were still sleeping peacefully, oblivious of the quandary in which their Officer and his batman found themselves.

Byrne made his second decision and the only one possible under the circumstances. He aimed his carbine at the animal, cocked it and whispered to Rice to shoot if it sprang or came forward – otherwise wait and see what happened. For what seemed a very long time they waited. To Byrne's intense relief and the equally intense disappointment of Rice, the glowing eyes vanished as the dark shape turned and vanished into the depths of the jungle.

Somewhat shaken, Byrne went back to his basha and Rice resumed his sentry duty. On waking the following morning, Byrne half-doubted what he had seen during the night. Had it actually been a tiger? Had there been anything there at all? Was the whole episode the result of a joint hallucination and would anyone believe him anyway? It was Rice himself who found the large paw marks in the soft sand on the edge of the stream that ran by the camp.

8 Platoon never did come across Seladang, though they found their tracks from time to time. The local police and planters spoke of Seladang with awe. These animals were wild cattle with an almost legendary reputation among the local population for aggressive behaviour, particularly towards the human race. C Company Platoon Commanders, between themselves, believed the lurid accounts of these wild and supposedly dangerous animals were greatly exaggerated for their benefit but were secretly glad no opportunity ever arose to test their theory.

Wild pigs unexpectedly crashing their way through the undergrowth when disturbed were a much more common occurrence. The first noise always caused guns to swivel and hearts to beat faster, until the source of the disturbance became obvious. The Platoon came across snakes rather less often.

Byrne saw his first snake very early one morning under inauspicious circumstances. The night before and for part of the morning in question, the Officers had entertained the Sergeants to drinks and a very hot curry. Though the Company was a close-knit community, it was only rarely that all the Officers and Sergeants were in camp at the same time. At such times, proper hospitality had to be extended. In turn, the two Messes traditionally vied with each other as to which could produce the hottest, often bordering on the inedible, curry. The chilli-strewn repast was inevitably accompanied by the drinking of large quantities of beer. Byrne had over-indulged. Not to the point of being incapable but, as he recollected remarking at the time, he had 'somewhat exceeded that elegant sufficiency' that was in order on such an occasion.

He did not feel in the least elegant later that morning and bitterly regretted the beer-for-beer bonhomie with his Platoon Sergeant that had marked the closing hours of the party. He had been woken from a fitful and sweaty sleep with an intense pain behind the eyes and a light-headedness which two aspirins had done nothing to alleviate. The outward cheerfulness of Sergeant Lennox, who was more used to such social occasions, made him feel little better as the Platoon assembled at 4.30 a.m. The small anti-malaria Paludrine tablets, which each member of the Platoon swallowed as a routine every morning, came close to choking him. The usually welcome drive in the cool of the early morning helped a little but he was in no particular mood to tackle bandits as the Platoon skirted some waste land near a kampong at the start of the patrol.

Byrne saw the snake first; some ten feet away and coiled on a small pile of brushwood. It was black and red and Byrne could have sworn it was other colours as well. He feared the worst and momentarily toyed with the idea of calling the patrol off on the grounds of his sudden illness. He was relieved when Spratt tapped him on the shoulder and pointed his Bren gun at the reptile. At least the snake wasn't the product of a fevered imagination brought on by the night's revels. The rest of the day Byrne sweated the headache away and almost enjoyed the all-in-stew washed down with hot strong tea that evening. At a later time he learnt from the local Police Inspector that the multi-coloured cause of alarm was very likely to have been the striped kukri snake.

Twice the Platoon encountered pythons. The first time some of them had very nearly trod on Malaya's largest snake. The Platoon was following up a single Typhoon air-strike on a small patch of jungle. The aircraft had fired its rockets in spectacular fashion and 8 Platoon went into the area. Contacting bandits was not considered likely and the whole minor operation seemed to Byrne to have been laid on to give the RAF some practice. They moved through the jungle alongside a small stream. Just as the rest of the Platoon, Byrne looked from side to side and occasionally down for signs of footprints. He was half-conscious of nearly standing on a very large frog. A pace or so later, realising he could not recollect having seen a frog in Malaya before, certainly not one as big, he turned to take a closer look at the amphibian. It was the recumbent head of a large python. The rest of the snake, or at least the fourteen feet or more that was visible, lay across the shallow stream and into the dark jungle undergrowth beyond. The leading scouts, moving up ahead on either side of the stream, surprisingly hadn't seen it. Neither had Corporal Grice who was following Byrne a few yards behind. Holding up his arm in the approved signal to halt, Byrne then pointed downwards. By this time Corporal Grice was himself almost standing on the snake's head. The expression of sheer horror on the face of the normally taciturn Yorkshire N.C.O. was something Byrne treasured for a long time. Clearly Corporal Grice had the same fear of snakes as himself. The rest of 8 Platoon needed little urging to make a short detour. The python, which continued to lay motionless across the stream, seemed oblivious to the sensation it had caused.

The second encounter with a python, probably larger than the first, happened when 8 Platoon were sweeping across a stretch of country in open order near a tin mine. It was a fine, clear day and the object of the exercise was to hearten the tin miners and show them the British Army was always on hand to protect them. The Platoon moved round the side of a hill; a gently sloping stretch of ground which was dotted with small bushes and trees. From his right Byrne clearly heard a stage whisper, obviously addressed to himself, from Private Rice, 'Can I kill it, Sir?' Standing in front of a bush, in and around which was coiled a very large python, stood the diminutive figure of Private Rice. His Sten gun pointing at the head of the python some two feet away, he urgently repeated his request. Meanwhile, the python showed no sign of concern at the grave danger it was in and remained disinterested and motionless. Some of the rest of the Platoon started to gather round to view the snake and were indignantly chased back into extended order by Sergeant Lennox.

Byrne had no intention of granting his batman's request and recollected that on at least one previous occasion Rice had shown an obvious hankering to wage a one-man war against the wildlife of Malaya. This time he wondered if there was an additional motive, that of money. Passing through a village the previous week, some of the Platoon had noticed that slices of snake were for sale in the Chinese butchers. Though expressing no wish to sample the delicacy, they had been impressed with the number of dollars being asked for each fillet. This manifestation of the eating habits of the local Chinese population had been the subject of some later discussion in the Platoon and had been found peculiar and infinitely less preferable to fish and chips. Nevertheless, the financial implications had obviously not been lost on Private Rice.

Byrne sympathised with Rice's wish to increase his income; a National Serviceman's pay, even including Local Overseas Allowance, was hardly princely. However, he was not enthusiastic. A shot would be heard a long way away and even Rice's quickly suggested alternative, bayonetting the snake, was not acceptable. He would reconsider, he said, providing enough men volunteered to carry the dead snake for the two days before the Platoon was due to return to base. Rice immediately volunteered but even Burton, who was always on the lookout for extra dollars to buy Woodbines, drew the line at carrying an increasingly more rotten dead python through the jungle for two days. Casting a last longing look at his once-intended victim, still coiled contentedly in the bush, Rice trotted after the rest of 8 Platoon. For days afterwards he frequently reminded the Platoon of the price such a python would have fetched in the local market, if only they had been more helpful.

Months later, Byrne had his own very personal contact with a snake, this time under more frightening circumstances than earlier encounters. 8 Platoon had been ordered to lay an ambush along the jungle edge overlooking a large rubber plantation. There had been vague reports of bandits in the area provided by the amateur but very enthusiastic members of the local Home Guard. As the Company Commander said, vague or unreliable information to act on was better than no information at all, so the Platoon was ordered to maintain an ambush in the area for three days. The local Home Guard, Byrne was assured, under some pretext or other would be ordered to remain behind the wire of their enclosed village for the three days.

Byrne and Sergeant Lennox decided to lay two ambushes. One was on the edge of the rubber with a clear view down the lines of trees. The other was by a well-used track they had discovered that ran parallel to the boundary of the plantation, 300 yards inside the jungle itself. A base camp was established, well away from both ambush positions. The Platoon rapidly settled itself into the then, by now, well-practised routine of guarding the base camp, observing from the ambush positions, regularly relieving those on ambush duty, periods of rest, cleaning weapons, unobtrusive feeding and generally keeping quiet.

Byrne was lying in the ambush overlooking the well-kept rubber estate along with six riflemen. It was a good position with a clear field of fire. In the recommended manner he had already been forward a little way out into the plantation and inspected the siting of each soldier from what would be the bandits' viewpoint if they should appear. He was satisfied that the section, for all practical purposes, was invisible in the dark shadows of the jungle edge, even though no member was more than two or three feet from open ground.

It was late in the afternoon of the second day of the ambush and they had settled in for another uneventful and long wait. The village was just out of sight and apart from a solitary rubber tapper in the distance that morning, they had seen no-one. Byrne stretched himself, relaxed and admired the shadows of the trees thrown on the lush green grass beneath by the weakening sun, enjoying that time of the day before the mosquitoes became irritatingly active.

The quiet of the afternoon was disturbed by voices coming from their right. 8 Platoon glimpsed khaki shirts as eight men rounded a slight bend and came into view, heading towards them, walking along the edge of the plantation. All were carrying shotguns. Safety catches were gently eased forward on the rifles and Bren gun but something was very wrong. The approaching group were all Malays, distinctive in their songkok pillbox hats. They cheerfully chatted to each other as they peered into the jungle from time to time and pointed their shotguns in a belligerent manner. Byrne recognised the Home Guard armlet, much the same as the one worn by the Local Defence Volunteers at the beginning of W.W.II. By now the carefree Home Guard Patrol was nearing the edge of the Platoon's position. There was too little time to move back into the jungle. A disaster was imminent. One untoward noise and eight shotgun blasts would have caused wounds and perhaps deaths. To have called out would almost certainly have had the same result. Byrne and the other petrified soldiers had already noticed many of the Home Guards' fingers were round the triggers of the shotguns. Byrne realised he had only one option and he knew his men were watching him, waiting for a lead, their faces showing the near-panic he felt himself. He gently lowered his carbine, buried his face into the ground and prayed. He knew his section would follow his example. Byrne guessed every man felt the same heavy, empty feeling in the pit of his stomach.

The Home Guard Patrol started to pass the ambush position, still happily chatting among themselves. They were no more than three yards in front of the prone and sweating members of the Platoon. Byrne, who was in the centre of the ambush, squinted upwards as far as he could without moving his head. He saw the plimsolled feet of the first man pass in front of him. So far, so good. Simultaneously he felt a squirming pressure across the back of his thighs. Fearing the worst and with difficulty controlling a violent urge both to be sick and sweep the offending creature away with his carbine, he risked twisting his neck and looked cautiously but quickly behind him. He saw a snake, greyish-brown in colour, undulating slowly across the back of his legs, just above the knees. It was probably no more than three or four feet long but to Byrne it seemed endless. It looked unpleasant and vicious. If he needed an additional incentive to keep still, this was it. To his immense relief, the snake showed no further interest in him, its tail flicked off his body and the reptile slid off into the jungle behind him and quickly disappeared. Meanwhile, the voices of the Home Guard had receded into the distance. A section of 8 Platoon breathed a collective heartfelt sigh of relief and Byrne's personal nightmare was over.

They knew it had been lucky for them that the Home Guard had treated their excursion as more of a social outing than an anti-bandit patrol. If they had been more vigilant and had seen the ambush, there would have been mayhem and 8 Platoon would have been the only loser. Byrne and Sergeant Lennox also speculated that it was even more lucky for the Home Guard that they had not walked into a bandit ambush rather than 8 Platoon.

Feeling physically and mentally drained after the experiences of the afternoon, that evening Byrne reported over the wireless what had happened in distinctly frosty terms. He suggested to the Company Commander that either the Home Guard were put under stricter controls or, if this was not possible and would give the game away, that the Platoon would be much safer if it was moved out of the area. The Company Commander, clearly relieved not to have a disaster on his hands, gave permission for the Platoon to pull out the following morning. This they did, keeping a careful lookout for any shotgun-carrying local inhabitants.

Byrne never did identify the snake which had been too close for comfort. However, the local Police Inspector did tell him the intrepid members of the offending Home Guard had been suitably admonished. Though they had understood their orders, it appeared that, in a not untypical Malay carefree manner, they had decided that a short walkabout outside the wire could do no harm!

Byrne only saw one more snake of any note, this time in even more dramatic circumstances than the encounter in the ambush. The Platoon had been given a rare afternoon and evening out in the local seaside resort. This was an occasional and popular event for the Platoon whose entertainment in camp was otherwise confined to drinking beer and eating banjos, the then equivalent of hamburgers, in the Indian Charwallah's marquee. The outing meant a two-hour each way truck journey. On arrival, the town being considered safe for off-duty soldiers of the Battalion to disport themselves unarmed, weapons were handed into the Police Station for safe storage where they were securely locked under guard in the cells. The members of 8 Platoon then went off to sample the delights of the town.

Byrne was usually free to enjoy himself, except when 8 Platoon had been detailed to find the Regimental Police patrol for the evening. This meant the wearing of his second-best uniform and the detailing off of four of his men who were given truncheons. Needless to say, this was not a popular duty. Though there was rarely much to do, the reluctant acting Regimental Policemen could think of much more pleasant things with which to occupy themselves than walking the streets, taking occasional looks into Chinese restaurants and bars to satisfy themselves the Yorkshire Fusiliers were behaving themselves. On the occasions that members of a certain neighbouring Scottish battalion were also in town, whose fighting qualities in the jungle were only equalled by their performance in the town's bars, Byrne insisted on joint patrols with his opposite number. This was on the advice of his Company Commander who had also advised that a bargain should be struck by the two Officers in charge, in that Scottish problems should be sorted out by Scots and Yorkshire problems by Yorkshiremen. There were times when Byrne mused on the soundness of this counselling as he stood outside a bar with his men and listened to the bangs, bumps and bad language coming from within, to be followed by an exodus through the door of heaving bodies and a red-faced Officer supervising his men hauling off loudly protesting Scottish soldiers for an enforced early return to their camp.

Byrne's favourite haunt was Suan Kee's. This was where the largest and most delicious king prawns he had ever tasted were served, topped with an equally appetising tomato sauce dressing. Followed by some special fried rice, chicken and several ice-cold Tuborg lagers, Malaya became the tropical paradise that one day would be described in travel brochures. Occasionally he would come across a planter he knew in the restaurant. This invariably had the happy outcome of a free meal, a chance to cement local relationships and of retaining more dollars in his wallet than he had anticipated.

On these outings, a few of the Platoon might buy tickets at the local New World Dance Hall, a rough equivalent to a Western nightclub, rather flashily decorated in a Chinese imitation of its American counterpart. The cabaret was almost invariably a demonstration by a pair of professional European dancers and drinks were expensive. The main attraction for the soldiers, almost entirely deprived of female company, was that the tickets were exchanged for quicksteps with 'taxi dancers'. These were the slim Chinese girl hostesses, all with raven-black hair, expressionless faces, dressed in silk, high-necked and slit from the thigh down, cheongsams. Chances of anything more than the strictly commercial ticket-a-dance arrangement in the New World Dance Hall were slim and it was rare for any member of 8 Platoon to return for a second visit, even if he could afford it.

8 Platoon found that most of the other attractions were definitely for the local population. The theatres with clashing gongs, colourful scenery and, to Western eyes, over-stylised performances had no more appeal than

cinemas showing Chinese or Asian films. Having taken in the sights and wandered round the small but teeming harbour, most of the Platoon contented themselves with a visit to one or more local bars and a curry or a Chinese meal; a change from jungle stews. What was strange to all the Platoon during these outings was the feeling of nakedness caused by not carrying a weapon. Carrying a rifle or S.M.G. whenever they went outside the Camp gates and sleeping with it by their side had become a habit. After their few precious hours of, in military parlance, 'rest and recreation', the Platoon reassembled at the appointed hour outside the Police Station to be reunited with their weapons and transport.

The night of Byrne's final confrontation with a snake, 8 Platoon was contentedly on its way back to base. Byrne was in the leading Land-Rover beside the driver. As was normal, all the vehicles were left open-topped. An ambush was not the time for passengers to leave a vehicle in an orderly fashion through the back. Stars shone in the dark sky and the almost cold night breeze was refreshing. Byrne had enjoyed an excellent meal and he was relaxed as the Platoon's vehicles purred along. Much later, he was told that, in the cool of the night, a snake might be attracted from the jungle or field to the residual warmth still being radiated by the open road, heat that had been stored there during the shimmering day. Byrne and his driver were not prepared for the sight of a gigantic king cobra reared to its full height a few yards in front of their approaching vehicle. In the dim headlights, the cobra appeared the most menacing sight Byrne had ever seen. There was not time to stop, even if Byrne or his driver had wanted to. They saw the hooded head appear to strike at them and almost touch the windshield before there was a loud slap as the Land-Rover struck the snake and whiplashed it onto the road. There was a mutual and unspoken understanding that they would not turn back to examine the dead reptile.

Chapter 7

Success

After a few weeks, Byrne found himself forgetting about animals and snakes. He no longer worried about stepping on a snake or coming face to face with a tiger round every bend in the track. Whenever he did meet a specimen of Malayan wildlife, it therefore came as an unexpected but pleasant surprise. So rare were these encounters that, disliking overmuch exaggeration, he was unable to embroider his letters home with very many stories of encounters with the fierce denizens of the jungle. He realised it had been naive of him to expect to come across large numbers of snakes, elephants and tigers the moment he set foot in the jungle. The Malayan jungle was not a zoo where the animals had no opportunity to get out of the way of unwanted visitors.

He did see crocodiles on several occasions. The first time was when the Platoon was wading up the shallows of an estuary alongside the bank and not far inland from the sea. Just ahead of them the leading scouts spotted some small crocodiles, three or four feet in length. They appeared to be harmless and not to harbour any aggressive intentions. On drawing Sergeant Lennox's attention to them, the dour Scot pointed out that the parents of these baby crocodiles, which could be three or four times larger, might turn out to be less friendly. Byrne whitened slightly, clutched his carbine a little more tightly and moved the Platoon's line of advance just a shade nearer to the river bank.

Though the sight of large animals or snakes was rare, the jungle was far from lifeless and never slept. There was always the unforgettable background noise of insects, often chattering gibbons and the all too frequent whine of mosquitoes. The Army had taken the trouble to provide the Platoon with a mosquito repellent. Byrne found it had an unattractive smell and also felt greasy and unpleasant when put on the skin. In a

60

perverse reaction, typical of the British soldier, 8 Platoon had long given up using it on the grounds that, far from repelling the winged nuisances, it attracted them. Byrne persevered for a while with the smelly liquid but eventually gave it up, coming to a more reasonable conclusion that, though the repellent might not attract mosquitoes, it did very little to discourage them.

Also available on free issue from a thoughtful War Department were tablets to keep the Platoon awake for long periods. Keeping alert, let alone awake, for hours on end, when in ambush, was always a problem, particularly during warm and muggy days. Once again the 8 Platoon expressed profound disagreement with the senior officers of the Royal Army Medical Corps and discarded this battlefield aid on the surprising grounds that the tablets sent them to sleep. Byrne found that, as far as he could tell, they made little difference to how sleepy he felt. He wondered if the War Office realised how little some of their well-intentioned efforts to provide medical solutions to practical problems were appreciated by ungrateful soldiers.

He did try, with considerable success, to take his predecessor's advice to make himself as comfortable as possible when on patrol. Atkins had firmly believed in the old Army adage that any fool could be uncomfortable. When on the move, much depended on a sensibly arranged and well-adjusted pack. Spare clothing against the back and any angular or hard objects as far away from the back as possible were essential. If fourteen or more days' rations had to be carried, the job of packing such a large number of tins required the most careful organisation.

Sleeping arrangements presented their own particular difficulties, difficulties that had to be solved if life was not to verge on the unbearable. The poncho one-man tent with spare mosquito netting hung over the ends kept him both water and mosquito-proof. The recommended regulation scrape for the hip was rarely successful and only useful for those who didn't move in their sleep. The softest underbrush that could be found put under a groundsheet, the latter preventing rising damp, completed Byrne's domestic preparations before turning in for the night. In spite of all these precautions, during the small hours Byrne occasionally thought, not of home, that was too remote, but longingly of his comparatively luxurious Army regulation bed and mosquito net cover back at camp. Sleep always came eventually. Come morning, there was nothing like a shave, followed by a wash in a clear cold stream and a mess tin of Sergeant Lennox's strong sweet tea to raise morale once again.

The Platoon had finished the second day of a seven-day sortie that was planned to finish with three days of ambushes. This was the longest operation so far for Byrne. Two weeks was about the maximum length 8 Platoon normally were away without an air drop, unless, as Sergeant Lennox said, you were prepared to break your back carrying tins of food. An obvious but welcome redeeming feature of a long patrol was, as the days went by, packs became slowly less of a burden. Byrne checked the sentries' positions and walked round the little camp to hear the latest whispered examples of Yorkshire humour. As usual, the Platoon was in excellent spirits. A stranger would have found little reason for this. Though unhealthily sallow in complexion, in reality the Platoon was remarkably fit. Spare flesh had long since disappeared. The unnaturally pallid appearance was entirely due to the many days the Platoon had spent under the shade of the jungle canopy.

The following morning, after their ablutions, the men breakfasted on tinned soya link sausages and Sergeant Lennox's tea. According to the Platoon Sergeant, whose word on such matters approached the force of law, it was unnecessary and timewasting to cater for individual tastes. The tea itself was always strong and 8 Platoon had to conform. The brew-up was made by boiling the water and then, in rapid succession, tipping in the tea, tinned milk and a tinful of sugar. The timing of the tipping and the length and rapidity of the subsequent stirring was an art Sergeant Lennox claimed to have mastered and to which no other member of the Platoon aspired. Any soldier brave enough to express a preference for tea without milk, sugar or both had to stand by with his mess tin, ready to dip it quickly into the dixie at the appropriate brief interval in the Sergeant's tea-making ceremony. Any such rare intruders into the brewing-up ritual were subject to a glare of disapproval from the master brewer himself.

The Platoon buried their empty tins, packed their belongings and checked their weapons. Meanwhile, Private Burton, the Platoon signaller, once again slung the aerial of his wireless high over some convenient branches prior to contacting Company Headquarters. Sergeant Lennox, for something to do, reminded everyone of the order of march. Byrne opened his map case, studied the coming days' route and worked out some preliminary compass bearings. Burton switched on the wireless and went through his twice-daily routine of a tuning and netting call to make contact with Company H.Q. 'Mike Bravo Mike Bravo Mike Bravo Mike Bravo Mike Bravo . . . tuning calls ends-net now.' He kept his finger down on the transmit button for the approved length of time. Burton hoped, that when he asked Company Headquarters 'how he was heard', meticulously using the correct voice procedure in case the Signals Sergeant was in a critical mood that morning, he would be rewarded with the familiar tones of the said Senior N.C.O. In his mind's eye he could visualise the Sergeant reclining at ease in the Company Signals Tent, eating eggs and bacon and drinking a civilised cup of tea. As was usual early in the morning, radio communications proved to be excellent. It was during the evening or night that atmospherics made the life of a Regimental Signaller intolerable and radio communications impossible. While Burton and the Signals Sergeant politely established their respective signal strengths, Byrne finished scribbling down his short situation report. It was boringly similar to all the others in recent weeks; nothing to report, a confirmation of their present position, the route they expected to follow that day and a map reference of where they hoped to be that night.

The next place they were aiming for, as Byrne had explained to the Platoon the evening before, was a point on the jungle edge next to a large Dunlop rubber estate. It was well up in the north of C Company's allotted operational area and had only been patrolled on a few occasions during the previous months. Life, it seemed was peaceful in that part of Malaya. The Battalion's Intelligence Officer had been told by his opposite number in the Police that there had been several rumours, unconfirmed by any tangible evidence, of a bandit presence in the area. Tangible evidence in Police terminology, usually meant burnings or killings. 'No more or less information than that', said the Company Commander to a rather disappointed Byrne, who had been hoping for something much more precise. Rather than showing the flag by touring round the estate looking warlike, C Company Commander continued, he had decided that some speculative ambushes in a few likely places might be more profitable. Byrne had no option but to agree with the reasoning. Though a very long shot, it was preferable to patrolling a rubber estate, either in a truck or on foot, in the vain hope that something would turn up. Byrne knew that any self-respecting bandit would almost certainly leave the area just as fast as he could if he thought the Security Forces were anywhere near. To try and get into the ambush areas unseen, he had taken the Platoon the long way round, a three-day left-flanking approach march through the jungle. 8 Platoon understood the tactics but wished their Commander would occasionally be less energetic.

That morning Byrne had noted there were four miles left to go as the crow flies; five, or possibly six in practice, as he well knew. However, the contours on the map were marked in convincing detail and he was confident he could get to the point he had selected, give or take a few hundred yards, without any difficulty. Burton, having sent the SITREP and exchanged a few daring irreverent final words with the Signals Sergeant,

centring round the hardships of the former compared with the easy camp
life of the latter, retrieved his aerial, hoisted the set on to his wide
shoulders and the Platoon was ready for the off.

Brockley and Hird as usual led the way, looking supremely professional
and no doubt feeling the part, with their jungle hats set at deliberately
rakish angles. They moved forward cautiously, stopping every now and
again to observe and listen. At intervals, one of the two would glance back
to see if the direction they were taking met with the approval of their
Platoon Commander. Byrne signalled minor corrections from time to
time. The jungle floor was almost clear of undergrowth, the slopes were
gentle and keeping direction was easy that morning.

The five miles or so to the edge of the jungle were covered without
incident. Not even the sudden noise of a wild pig thrashing in panic-
stricken flight from human intruders disturbed the calm. 8 Platoon quietly
made their way over the soft jungle floor in the comparative cool of the
early morning, enjoying the shade of the jungle canopy, well over 100 feet
above them. Even so, familiar dark patches of sweat still stained their
shirts. There was little in the way of dense undergrowth in which bandits
could hide themselves, or any steep gradients to claw their way up or slide
their way down; patrolling was almost a relaxing exercise for 8 Platoon
that morning.

In the distance, the sunlight near the tops of the trees became brighter
and the undergrowth became thicker. The leading scouts could see a mass
of thick vegetation which marked either a clearing or perhaps the beginning of the rubber estate which they were seeking. Without waiting for
orders, Brockley and Hird automatically stopped and crouched down. So
in turn did the rest of the Platoon, facing outwards in a position of all-
round defence. Byrne went cautiously forward with Rice just behind him;
he laid down, wriggled his way through the few feet of long grass and
carbine first, peered round the trunk of a substantial tree.

The tree was almost on the edge of a narrow brown laterite road that ran
along the edge of the jungle, beyond which was a typical Dunlop rubber
estate. The sun shone on serried ranks of well-spaced rubber trees as far as
the eye could see, set in what, from a distance, looked like a well-tended
village green. Byrne could see nothing unusual. Placing three fingers
against his arm, Byrne gave the signal for Sergeant Lennox to come
forward. Quietly they discussed the situation and they agreed that, for all
practical purposes, they were where they wanted to be. There was nothing
human or animal in sight but, in the absence of any obvious alternative,
this was where they would start operations. Byrne sent Rice back to bring

forward Spratt and his Bren gun plus three riflemen and Corporal Grice. Corporal Grice and the riflemen were positioned on either side of Spratt near the tree. Sergeant Lennox collected another five members of the Platoon and led them 100 yards to the left to set up a similar position near what appeared to be traces of an old narrow track that led back into the jungle from the road.

Meanwhile, Byrne moved quietly back several hundreds of yards into the trees with the rest of the Platoon to establish a base for the night. He selected the most suitable position he could find, a convenient hillock surrounded by enough foliage to help conceal a bivouac area. Sentries were posted and the Platoon was given his standard short lecture on the importance of track discipline and keeping quiet. A brew-up was authorised. Domestic duties completed, he made his way back to Corporal Grice's position to supervise operations during what promised to be an uneventful afternoon.

Lying back in the shadows, Byrne unscrewed the top of his water-bottle and downed a long draught of warm 'jungle juice'. This was a yellowy-green acidic liquid made by dissolving Army-issued lime crystals in water. Opinions on the merits of this supposedly refreshing and health-giving drink were divided. Some of the Platoon enjoyed it; even to the extent of occasionally drinking it when in camp when their beer money had run out. Others, with perhaps more sophisticated tastes, refused to drink it at any time, swearing it would dissolve their stomach walls. Byrne enjoyed its bitter-sweet taste. Though not meant to be a substitute, he much preferred jungle juice to water treated with purification tablets which gave it an unnatural and unmistakable flavour of chlorine.

The hours went slowly by. No animals or birds stirred. The tappers had obviously already finished their work before 8 Platoon had arrived. Byrne changed over the men in the two positions at mid-afternoon and resisted the temptation to relieve the monotony by taking a section to explore along the boundaries of the rubber estate which swept away in broad curves to left and right. Ambushes they had been sent to lay and ambushes it had to be. Patience and the occasional somewhat grudging acceptance of orders, that didn't always seem to make too much sense when actually in the jungle, were things both he and the Platoon had long since acquired.

Night came quickly and as the more distant rubber trees started to fade rapidly in the darkness, Byrne decided that they had done enough for King and Country for one day. A good night's sleep followed by ambushes in position before first light would be more likely to pay dividends than sitting in the blackness on the million to one chance a bandit might decide to go for a midnight stroll. The Platoon retired to their temporary base for the evening meal. Byrne was satisfied, as far as he ever could be certain of anything in Malaya where jungle walls had ears, that the Platoon had not been detected. On the other hand, the Platoon was only too aware that they themselves had seen nothing. At Byrne's request, Burton reported this unexciting news over the radio to the Signals Sergeant. In turn he was told there were no changes in the original orders and that the ambushes should continue. The sentries round the small camp gazed at the dark shapes of the trees around them and looked forward to being relieved while, to the eternal whine of mosquitoes, the rest of the Platoon settled down to sleep.

8 Platoon were up and about well before dawn. Without exhibiting undue enthusiasm, the original teams were back in their ambush positions as the first warmth of the sun bathed the rubber trees and the green grass in front of them, eventually filtering a little into their leafy camouflaged positions. Two hours went by and nothing disturbed the peace of the countryside. The tappers, who normally started work early, clearly began their labours somewhere else on the estate. Then, in the distance, two Chinese tappers appeared. Working their way quickly from tree to tree, they emptied the small pots of latex into their containers and then, with deft swift strokes, cut a new surface on the groove round the tree to make it produce more rivulets of white sticky liquid. This appearance of human life was the most exciting event of the day or, for that matter, of the whole patrol so far.

Byrne and the section watched the tappers intently, confident that they were invisible to the unsuspecting Chinese. It was Rice, the last man on the right of their ambush position, who saw the bandits first.

Walking directly towards the tappers from the right and only twenty yards away from the busy Chinese, were two khaki-clad figures. Byrne inwardly cursed himself for not seeing them earlier, so intent he had been in watching the tappers. To his chagrin he realised the bandits must have walked at least seventy yards from the jungle edge before they had been seen by Rice. The tappers by now had themselves seen the bandits. They stood together by a tree looking somewhat apprehensively at the ap-proaching figures. They were the first live bandits Byrne had seen. Both carried what appeared to be Lee Enfield rifles and wore rather baggy khaki hats with a peak and a red star on the front – the hallmark of typical members of the M.R.L.A.

The two bandits stopped and started to talk with the tappers. Though still holding on to their rifles, they appeared to be totally relaxed and oblivious to any possible danger. Byrne and his small section were far from relaxed. He briefly wondered whether his men also felt a cold, sinking feeling in the stomach and sweat running down inside their shirts. The immediate problem was only too obvious. Though only about fifty yards away, they could hardly open fire with two unarmed and possibly innocent civilians so close to the bandits. Byrne shuddered at the thought of having to explain two dead civilians at the local police station. In addition, the trees between them and the section position would make the whole thing, in any case, very much a hit and miss affair. Byrne reasoned that the bandits would be very likely to re-enter the jungle by the same way they had come, some 100 yards or so to their right. If this guess was correct, it would be logical to move back and to work quietly well to the right and find a position with a good field of fire where there would be no danger to the tappers. Logical perhaps, if there was not the possibility of other bandits crouched down at the jungle edge covering their comrades and awaiting their return. Byrne squirmed forward as far as he dared and looked right. He could only see a short distance along the jungle edge from his prone position. There was no sign of life in the undergrowth or among the trees but he was well aware there could be others, as well as 8 Platoon, lying in the shadows. Something had to be done and quickly before all opportunity was lost. Byrne tapped Spratt, the Bren Gunner, on the shoulder. Spratt, diverted from his task of trying to keep at least one of the khaki figures in his sights as the bandits moved around, looked up. Byrne signalled for him to pull back. Quietly they moved twenty yards to the right to where there was a clear but narrow lane between the rubber trees to the front. Spratt having settled in behind his Bren, Byrne brought up the others. Though there was little physical effort, Byrne and the section were sweating profusely as they peered carefully between the long grass at the group of four figures still talking animatedly among the rubber trees. Byrne whispered in Spratt's ear to open fire as soon as a target appeared in the gap to his front and motioned to the others to do the same when the first shot was fired.

He was only just in time. Whether some sixth sense told the bandits something was amiss or whether they thought they had spent too long in the open, they abruptly turned away from the tappers and swiftly started to walk back the way they had come. Byrne was conscious, in the few seconds it took the bandits to cover the ground between the tappers and his quickly selected field of fire, that the bandits were walking one behind the other and a few yards apart. A disappointment, as only one would appear as a target for the Bren. As the first bandit appeared from behind a tree Spratt fired. Not in approved short bursts but in the excitement, one long burst which seemed to go on forever. He emptied the magazine. Byrne thought Spratt had missed when he saw the first strike of the bullets hit the ground near the base of the tree the first bandit had just passed but as the bullets of the over-long burst started to go high and wide to the right the bandit fell over, well and truly dead, with two bullet holes in the side of his chest. Byrne and the rest of the section fired away at the second bandit, while Spratt changed his prematurely empty magazine, until their own magazines were empty. The bandit ran on, dodging in and out among the trees, eventually disappearing into the jungle away to the right, apparently unharmed. The section swore he must have covered the 100 yards in better than even time.

Sergeant Lennox and the rest of the Platoon arrived. They were despatched after the remaining bandit though Byrne thought the pursuit would be fruitless, as it turned out to be. The bandit could be 50 or 500 yards away laid up in the jungle. Either way they wouldn't find him. The tappers had not moved except to lay down behind the nearest tree. They appeared to be heartily relieved they had not joined the dead bandit laying sprawled on the grass still clutching his rifle. Those who had not gone chasing after the remaining bandit with Sergeant Lennox gathered round the body, unashamedly pleased with their success. The many weeks of tramping through the jungle, sweating in ambushes and being pestered by swarms of mosquitoes at last seemed to have been worthwhile.

Lofty Burton threw his aerial over the branches of the nearest rubber tree and went through the routine of contacting the ever-listening Company Headquarters. Byrne gingerly searched the body. Apart from the rifle, the bandit was carrying two small Japanese hand grenades. There were a handful of .303 cartridges in a bandolier round his waist but disappointingly, the bandit had not been carrying any papers. He did, to Byrne's surprise, have three expensive Parker pens in his shirt pocket and a surprising number of dollar notes. On return from his fruitless pursuit, Sergeant Lennox managed to persuade Byrne, without too much difficulty, that it would be both unnecessary and a great shame to hand over all the pens and dollars to the local Police, hinting darkly that that would be the last they would see of them. It did not take very long for a Scot and a Yorkshireman to decide that charity began at home. Most of the money was tucked away in Lennox's pocket to fund the inevitable Platoon celebration party that evening. Though it was hardly necessary, a guard was put on the two very subdued tappers and the Platoon waited for Lofty to establish wireless contact.

The Company Commander was highly delighted at the Platoon's success, or so Lofty's friend the Signals Sergeant said. But it would be at least two hours before the Platoon could be picked up as the Company's transport was already out dropping off 7 Platoon at the start of another patrol. To pass the time, Byrne ordered a brew-up while he and Sergeant Lennox tried out their elementary interrogation techniques in even more elementary Malay on the cowed and unenthusiastic tappers. They met with no success. Yes, the bandits had been talking to them – they had not recognised them – they had not seen the two bandits before – in fact, they were adamant they hadn't seen any bandits before – they wanted nothing to do with bandits – they could not remember one word that the bandits had said. Byrne decided they were so frightened that further questioning would only result in the tappers denying the very existence of the State of Emergency and that further interrogation was best left to the experts.

Three hours later, the trucks arrived. Brockley and Hird tied the bandit by his wrists and feet to a thick branch and gingerly loaded him onto a flat truck. 8 Platoon handed the bandit into the police station in the nearest village, not forgetting on the way there to point out to curious spectators the inevitable fate of all bandits. The Platoon party that night was a tremendous success, the Charwallah and his assistants, revelling in the extra business, excelled themselves in both the quantity and the heat of the curry and the coldness of the bottles of lager.

It was many days later that C Company was told that the dead bandit was Ah Wah, a one-time rubber tapper from Johore who had gone into the jungle to join the M.R.L.A. eighteen months previously. It appeared he was of no significance in the communist hierarchy. Nevertheless, as the Company Commander said, the bandits were less one soldier, one rifle, two grenades and he strongly suspected, several dollars.

Chapter 8

Bombardments

Byrne ate a leisurely breakfast and strolled round the camp in the warm sunshine. The two other Platoons had been out on patrol for several days. They were both expected back that afternoon and then it would be 8 Platoon's turn, after enjoying a forty-eight-hour break from operations, once again to start missing comfortable nights in soft beds under the welcome protection of mosquito nets.

He met Sergeant Lennox, who was also taking the morning air. As they walked along they watched the members of their Platoon sitting outside their tents variously smoking, talking, writing letters home or cleaning their weapons. Lennox made approving noises in broad Scottish accents at the last-mentioned. The Dhobiwallah passed by, balancing a large bundle of washing on his head. He did not forget to enquire whether Byrne Sahib and Lennox Sahib had been satisfied with yesterday's laundry. The Charwallah, seeing two important people in the Company's hierarchy passing by his canteen tent flap, in the interests of good commercial relations invited them in for a cup of early morning coffee. The stillness of the morning as they drank the dark, very strong coffee, was only disturbed by a crashing of gears as Private Gingell drove off to collect the daily water.

It was the Signal Sergeant's turn on listening watch. Though the next fixed times to contact Battalion Headquarters and the two Platoons on operations were some hours away, he sat with two sets of headphones round his neck, in a comfortable cane chair outside the Signals Tent, waiting for any urgent unscheduled messages. He had summoned Burton, 8 Platoon's signaller, ostensibly to brush up his Slidex, the Army's method of encoding map references. This lesson had somehow turned into the Sergeant reading extracts from a three-week-old edition of the

Yorkshire Post on the current state of Leeds United. Burton, a keen Middlesbrough supporter, tried to appear interested.

Two Company Cooks passed by carrying a large and anonymous piece of meat between them and announced their intention of making a curry for Sunday lunch. Rice, overhearing this remark, as he tried to persuade the Company Quartermaster Sergeant to let him have one of the brand new Sten guns that had just arrived in exchange for his old one, said he was not surprised to hear this as making roast beef and Yorkshire puddings required some degree of cooking skill.

The Company Clerk arrived to present the Company Commander's compliments and would Mr. Byrne and Sergeant Lennox please come along to the Ops Room to talk about the next patrol. 8 Platoon had rarely been involved in operations with artillery, though Byrne was aware a Battery of 25-pounders was always available if they were called upon to support C Company. They had seen the guns in action from time to time, either in support of some grandiose operation or practising their skills by firing into those parts of the jungle where bandits might just conceivably be in camp or passing through the area. Whether this harassing fire actually did harass the enemy, 8 Platoon had reservations. The Platoon had been deployed on two occasions when they could hear the guns rumbling in the distance. These had only resulted in what the Platoon regarded as unnecessary mosquito bites as they waited in vain in ambush positions for terrified bandits to run across their front.

On one unforgettable patrol, 8 Platoon had the undivided attention of two Batteries of 25-pounders. The Company Commander and Byrne wondered, after the event, if the operation, organised by Battalion Headquarters, was inspired more by a planner's vivid imagination or by the fact that the Gunner C.O. had no other calls on his services that day and the Gunners were becoming bored. The plan was that the guns would shell the site and the general area of a suspected bandit camp, following which 8 Platoon would move into the area and see what they could see. The fact that the operation would only require twenty-four men and that this was not normally considered the most effective way of attacking a bandit camp, appeared to confirm suspicions that the alleged information was vague, to say the least. If this was the case, Byrne thought, it was a pity the Gunner Officer wasn't also given the less glamorous job of ploughing through the jungle, making camp and getting up at three in the morning to be on the start-line in time; instead of firing the guns from a school playing field in front of an admiring local population and being back in camp for lunch.

The approach march to the area Byrne had selected for the camp actually turned out to be pleasant. It was cool under the green canopy and there was little undergrowth to make progress difficult through the well-spaced tall trees of the primary jungle. The Platoon made camp above a small clear stream with fresh clean sand on either bank, which ran through a sunlit glade reminiscent of woods back home, except that the tropical green of the jungle was more glowingly luxuriant than anything found in temperate climates. Byrne always got a thrill from thinking that it was more than possible such places had not been seen by human eyes before and wondered if this pleasure was shared by any of his Platoon.

His orders for the following day were both clear and straightforward. The start-line was two miles away and 8 Platoon had to be on it by 9.00 a.m. The target was less than a mile farther on, just over the other side of a long, high hill with steep sides. The shelling of the hoped-for bandit camp was to start at 10.00 a.m. and to continue till 10.30 a.m., at which time 8 Platoon was to advance over the top and search the area. Byrne was confident he knew exactly where he was and that the Platoon was in the right place. The stream near where they had pitched camp overnight was marked on the map; the shape of the contour lines and the narrow distances between them clearly indicated a long, high hill with steep sides. Establishing the whereabouts of the crest of a hill precisely was never easy and often impossible, from a vantage point at the bottom of a valley. However, Byrne deployed the Platoon on the valley floor on either side of a small waterfall which cascaded down the steep side of the hill. The waterfall, Byrne idly mused, resembled a smaller edition of High Force on the River Tees. The Platoon sat down to wait, clutching their weapons and encouraged by Sergeant Lennox to keep their eyes and ears open, just in case a terror-stricken bandit did appear.

Byrne was still thinking nostalgically of the River Tees and his last visit there with his girlfriend when the first shell fell, on the dot at 10.00 a.m., 300 yards away, to their front and on 8 Platoon's side of the hill. The second landed a few seconds later. It came whistling in from the left and exploded much nearer to the, by now, deeply concerned members of the Platoon. Normal procedure should have been to call up the Company on the radio and, through them, correct the fall of shot in the approved manner taught at Eaton Hall. Byrne, in little more than a split second, decided there was no time for such niceties and with a shout of 'follow me!' led his men downstream, low-hurdling the boulders and at the fastest stumbling speed the stream bed permitted. He ignored the idyllic surroundings he had so recently admired. A quarter of a mile downstream and to his relief hearing the shells exploding farther and farther behind, Byrne stopped to catch his breath. Surrounded by the Platoon, gasping after their unexpected exertions, he wondered whether he would go down in the Regiment's history as the first officer to lead his men away from the sound of the guns – a crime made even more heinous by the fact that the retreat had been at a pace verging on the panic-stricken.

Having put even more distance between the Platoon and the start-line, on which, from the noise, the Field Batteries were still putting down a most impressive stonk, Byrne told Burton to put up his aerial. Private Burton was not, hardly surprising under the circumstances, in a good humour. Complaining that, as the wireless set had bumped its way through his back and into his chest, he would be surprised if any valves were still working and that he would be taking an early opportunity of leaving the signalling profession to become an ordinary infantryman, he expressed surprise that his first tuning and netting call resulted in him hearing the cheerful loud and clear voice of the Signals Sergeant. Following a request to 'Fetch Sunray', Byrne was able to tell the Company Commander of his doubts as to the competence of the Gunners at map reading, or alternatively, if they were able to understand a map, their ability to point their guns in the right direction and whose side were they on anyway? The Company Commander ordered 8 Platoon to return to camp. He described the situation to the Battery Commander and enquired, in somewhat more diplomatic terms than Byrne had used, what had happened. He was told that the guns had been pointing in the right direction and that the problem undoubtedly lay with the inability of not over-bright Infantry Platoon Commanders to tell one side of a hill from another. On his return, Byrne seethed. The argument continued until late evening with much exchanging of map references, until the Commanding Officer called a halt to the mutual recriminations by declaring that both his soldiers and the Royal Artillery had conducted themselves with the utmost professionalism and that the unfortunate incident was because of an error in the map. So honour was satisfied all round at Officer level. Burton, however, with strong support from the rest of the Platoon, expressed the fervent hope that, in future, the next victims of the long-range snipers would be bandits.

Byrne's next dealing with the Royal Regiment was a theoretical one. The Brigade Commander decided that, though the Officers were of necessity concentrating on the arts of jungle warfare, it was important that they did not forget the tactics that would be employed in a war in Europe. He therefore decreed that there would be a one day T.E.W.T. (Tactical

Exercise Without Troops) to be held at Brigade Headquarters. Each Battalion and Supporting Arm would provide representatives. C Company's share in this event would be one Officer.

The Company Commander and the 2i/c, being older soldiers and worldly wise, decided that they would inevitably be far too busy to attend and that who would be better to represent the Company than the most recently trained and junior subaltern. Hence it was Byrne who found himself getting up early one morning to don his best uniform, socks and puttees, to be driven the eighty miles to Brigade Headquarters, unsure whether to feel flattered or to bemoan his lack of seniority.

The Brigade Study Period was little different from any military study period before or since. There were comfortable armchairs in the front rows, reserved for the more senior officers attending. They could be asked to comment on the proceedings but were unlikely to be asked questions. The more junior officers, who were very likely to be asked questions, were directed to hard seats in rows behind their betters. Byrne found himself, to his relief, sitting at the back on, in military parlance, what was known as a Chair, Folding Flat. Unused for many months to sitting in class, feeling the effects of the early start and enjoying the rest after weeks of strenuous physical exercise in the jungle, the hardness of the chair did not prevent Byrne drifting into an occasional state of semi-consciousness. Though reasonably well versed in Platoon tactics in conventional warfare, and with a passable knowledge of responsibilities at the dizzying heights of commanding a Company, he found himself bewildered by the myriad of problems associated with the handling of one Division, let alone two. Though recognising many of the names of the Arms and Services, during the decreasing number of periods when he was paying attention as the temperature in the room steadily rose, he marvelled at the complexities of the logistics and tactics involved with the deployment of Engineer Regiments, Armoured Brigades and the rest of BAOR's impressive Order of Battle; a far cry from deciding the best place to site the Bren gun in an ambush. The place names were even less familiar; the significance of Hameln, the Minden Gap and the Weser was a closed book to Byrne. His inadequacy was reinforced by the occasional sage noddings of the senior officers in the front seats as the 'school solutions' were revealed by the Brigadier and the battle progressed. Byrne was, however, certain that war had been declared, that the Russians were advancing and the British Army was going backwards.

Byrne was slowly emerging from a reverie when he heard the Brigadier say, 'Given the situation as shown, where should we put the three Gunner

Field Regiments?' He tapped the large map on the wall behind him and then consulted the seating plan on his lectern. Obviously this was a difficult question, fraught with complex tactical problems, as the senior officers in the front looked very intelligent but did not volunteer an opinion. The Brigadier, having scanned the list of names, looked up and said, 'Byrne, what do you think?' Byrne got smartly to his feet, fervently wishing he was anywhere but where he was, briskly walked to the map and looked at it in what he hoped was a professional manner. The red hieroglyphics, he thought, must be the enemy and the blue, friendly forces. He did not dare examine the scale of the map at the bottom as he should have known this already and to make matters worse, he could not remember the range of a 25-pounder. Making sure he was on that part of the map marked with blue symbols, he selected the reverse slopes of a light brown range of hills, picked up the pointer and waved it over as large an area as he thought military propriety would allow. The senior officers showed no trace of emotion as they looked at the Brigadier to find out whether they should look approving or otherwise. To his relief the Brigadier didn't ask him the reasons for his choice and as there seemed to be no further call on his services, Byrne walked smartly back to his seat and waited in trepidation. The Brigadier closely examined the area of the map which had just been so liberally indicated. After some seconds of earnest contemplation, which seemed an age to Byrne, the Brigadier pronounced that, though that particular range of hills was not the one he had had in mind, siting the guns there did have certain advantages as well, of course, as disadvantages but was certainly a suggestion worthy of consideration. He asked the Commanding Officer of the Brigade's Field Regiment for his view. Rising slowly and impressively to his feet, the Gunner C.O. said that, though the particular range of hills in question was not the one that had immediately sprung to his mind, siting the guns there did have advantages as well as some disadvantages. He was firmly of the opinion that the suggestion merited consideration. Other senior officers followed, unanimous in the view that there were advantages and disadvantages and with equally firm opinions that the suggestion should be seriously considered. Byrne breathed an inward sigh of relief. The curry lunch, served on china plates on crisp white table cloths with ice-cold lagers in the Brigade Officers' Mess under the cooling air of the revolving fans in the ceiling, had never tasted better.

8 Platoon met the Cavalry the following week for the first time. A troop of scout cars from one of the British Army's better known Regiments was occupied in a 'showing the flag' tour of the towns and villages in the

Battalion's area. Byrne and the Platoon were walking back to the Company base through the neighbouring local village, having completed a three-day patrol, also with the intention of impressing the populace with their warlike appearance and so assuring them of security. In their bedraggled and sweat-stained jungle greens, they felt envious of the Cavalry's smartly green-painted reconnaissance vehicles, highlighted with resplendent brightly coloured Regimental Crests and equally jealous of the well-pressed uniforms of the occupants.

The subaltern commanding the troop hailed Byrne in that cheerful and friendly manner to be expected from an officer in a senior Cavalry Regiment. He complained of the boring nature of his duties. It appeared that showing the flag was even more boring than escorting senior officers and the occasional convoy and how much he envied the infantry chaps who were really soldiering. In short, he would love to see some action and could Byrne think of anything he might shoot at? Byrne was helpful. There was, he said, an old bandit camp near the top of a large jungle-covered hill that overlooked the village. The Platoon had stumbled across it by accident many weeks earlier. The Troop Commander expressed surprise, common to many non-footsloggers, that a camp could be so close. It was a frequent misconception that all bandit camps were far away in the depths of the jungle. Byrne pointed out the location of the camp as near as he could remember and suggested that if they wanted to fire at something, there was as good a place as any. Profuse in his thanks, the Troop Commander consulted his map and gave out his orders. The barrels of the little 2-pounder guns moved quickly upwards, to the right and pointed towards the top of the hill. Firing began to gasps of amazement from the, by now, large and hugely impressed audience of small children. 8 Platoon tramped away down the main road of the village, watching the puffs of smoke as the little shells landed on what was almost certainly a deserted patch of jungle.

The friendly pops of the bombardment faded as the Platoon passed the Police Post guarding the gap in the wire that surrounded the village. Byrne remembered being told at O.C.S. that the Infantry was the Queen of the Battlefield. Walking the last few miles back to Camp in the sweltering humidity of the midday sun he concluded that, though 8 Platoon might be the Queen of the Battlefield, the glamour normally associated with Royalty was not always theirs.

Looking for business was not always confined to the Royal Artillery. C Company Commander had been badgered by the Support Company Commander for some days to find useful work for the Mortar Platoon. Though this Platoon frequently left their 3 inch Mortars behind and acted as ordinary infantry, they did like to keep their hands in. Without the range of 25-pounders, their usual role was one of mortaring likely tracks or crossing places near the jungle edge as suggested by the Battalion Intelligence Officer or the Police. After several pointed requests, the Company Commander decided it would be churlish not to find something for the Mortars to do. He delegated Byrne to consult with the Officer i/c Mortars and come up with a plan for his approval.

Byrne first talked it over with the Platoon Sergeant. A minor operation with a simple plan was called for. Neither of them were overly enthusiastic at the prospect of a complex operation to give the Mortar Platoon practice. They wanted particularly to avoid a plan which would require the Platoon to go chasing around the jungle fringes for hours on end on a wild goose chase; especially as the Mortars would be comfortably ensconced in a static baseplate position, no doubt fortified at frequent intervals by mess tins of tea.

The plan they produced was simplicity itself and was approved by the Mortar Platoon Commander and both Company Commanders, virtually without change. Only six miles from Camp was a badly overgrown rubber plantation. It was situated between the jungle edge and a well-kept Dunlop estate. The few tracks crossing this tangled mass of old trees and undergrowth provided an excellent approach for any bandit who wished to contact the tappers at work. The fire plan was straightforward and based on a principle much used in larger scale operations. First there would be concentrated linear mortar fire along the edge of the overgrown rubber. The fire would then lift and move in bounds across the area, finishing on a line some 100 yards or so into the jungle. Beyond the finishing line would be 8 Platoon. The Platoon was to be split into two ambush parties, each watching one of the more distinct tracks that ran through the old rubber plantation and into the jungle itself. The whole business would last twenty minutes. Towards the end of this period, as many more senior commanders had fondly hoped in the past of operations on a considerably more grandiose scale, the theory was that 8 Platoon would have the easy task of shooting terrified bandits as they bolted along the tracks to avoid the lethal creeping barrage behind them. The whole idea reminded Byrne of the days he had spent in his youth watching his Father and friends gathered round a warren with their shotguns, waiting for the rabbits to flee from their burrows to avoid the pursuing ferrets. There were some essential differences, thought Byrne; it was known that rabbits were there and they were much more predictable than bandits.

The previously agreed map references were confirmed by signal to Support Company the day before the operation. The Mortar Platoon Officer was to establish his baseplate position shortly before midday when the first bomb was to be fired. 8 Platoon was to set off well before dawn, debus unobtrusively some miles away from the scene of the intended action, work their way into the jungle till they came across the tracks, turn left, cautiously move down them and select their ambush positions.

It was a very hot and humid day. Even under the jungle canopy, their jungle greens were black with sweat. Corporal Grice complained of a sore crotch, Private Rice had a headache and recently promoted Lance Corporal Spratt announced that the straps that supported the Bren gun were cutting into his shoulders. Sergeant Lennox shut them up with the remark calculated to annoy all National Servicemen, that if they had wanted an easy life they shouldn't have volunteered. The tracks were easily found. They were not far apart and Byrne led the Platoon down one of them towards the jungle edge. The paths had been little used and from marks on the ground in the wetter parts, the only visible tracks were those of wild pig; the distinctive impression of the rubber soles of the boots beloved by bandits were nowhere to be seen.

The dark green haze ahead grew lighter as they approached the jungle edge. The primary jungle stopped abruptly, the track ran down into an overgrown ditch that had once divided it from the rubber plantation. Beyond the ditch was a tangled mass of grey and white old rubber trees, some long since fallen and now slowly disintegrating. Long grass, thorns, bush and rotting vegetation filled in the gaps between. Byrne checked his watch and noted there was an hour to go before midday. Sergeant Lennox and the two leading scouts went off along the jungle edge. They were back within a few minutes to report the second track was only 100 yards away and if anything, seemed even less used than the one they had just followed. Byrne decided to wait a little longer before they moved back along the tracks to lay their ambushes. He consulted his Army-issue watch again. This was one piece of precision equipment about which there were no complaints and of which the C.Q.M.S. kept a close record, leaving no chance for a subaltern to overlook handing his in when he was eventually posted back to the U.K.

With just a few minutes to go before the first mortar bombs were due, Sergeant Lennox and his section moved off towards the other track. They were not yet out of sight when the first mortar bombs fell – a few hundred yards into the jungle behind 8 Platoon. The crumps of the bombs exploding were as menacing as they were near. There was no doubt in the minds of the Platoon as to what was happening, the Mortars were firing on the finishing line and were apparently intent on shooting the fire plan backwards. There was no alternative. With a distinct feeling of *déjà vu*, Byrne shouted brief instructions to Sergeant Lennox who, an alarmed expression on his face, was already hurrying back. Leaping over fallen trees and crashing through the undergrowth, Brockley and Hird led the Platoon down the track. The sound of the exploding 3 inch mortar bombs receded but then became louder as the barrage lifted and moved to deposit its shrapnel closer to the heels of the fleeing soldiers. Byrne pounded his way along behind the leading scouts, collecting his share of the bruised shins and face scratches that were being liberally distributed among the Platoon. Byrne was acutely conscious of the total indignity of the situation and did not dare even think of what was happening to his reputation as a Platoon Commander in the minds of his men. However, even when in full flight, he found some humour in wondering what any bandits fleeing from the mortars along the track would have made of being passed by 8 Platoon.

Fortunately there were no bandits. The Platoon's initial turn of speed left the moving barrage sufficiently far behind to allow for a more sedate pace. Sergeant Lennox raised their spirits by remarking that he had heard nothing of the problems of Corporal Grice's crotch, Rice's headache or Spratt's shoulder straps during the last few minutes. The Platoon left the overgrown rubber, moved well into the immaculate Dunlop estate and brewed-up.

C Company did receive an apology. The chinagraph start and finish lines on the map had somehow been misread and Support Company were much relieved there had been no casualties. In retrospect, the Platoon thought that, though running through the Malayan countryside pursued by falling missiles from one's own Mortar Platoon, who even wore their cap badge and not a Gunner one, was not an occupation that had any appeal. The incident had not been entirely without humour. A view reinforced by four crates of lager from the Mortar Platoon Officer that arrived on the next truck from Battalion Headquarters.

Chapter 9

Sport, Social Life and the Adjutant

Even during the Emergency there were occasional social and sporting events. From time to time there were minor celebrations in the Company Officers', Sergeants' and Other Ranks' Messes. It was only rarely that all five of the C Company's Officers were in camp. When they were, it was usually marked by an above-average dinner. They had long ceased to rely on Ah Ling, their Cantonese Chinese Cook to produce anything other than the just edible. He was a very plump, willing, happy soul but incapable of producing anything more complex than passable bacon and eggs. The Company Commander was convinced that the War Department (Malayan Branch) mistakenly believed anyone with a Chinese name could cook and made their appointments accordingly. This was a view confirmed by the Company's Chinese interpreter, who more than once confided in him that Ah Ling would be lucky to be employed as a washer-up even in a second-rate Malacca Chinese restaurant. However, the Charwallah who ran the Company Canteen could always be relied upon to produce a superb chicken curry which, washed down with cold lager, made an excellent prelude to an after-dinner game of mah-jong.

Though opportunities to entertain the local dignitaries and planters were rare because of the difficulty in raising a quorum of Officers, occasional individual invitations from local Police Officers and planters to Sunday lunch were much welcomed. Planters and their wives could be relied upon to produce spectacular Indian or Malay curries, served on china plates on snow-white table cloths under a cooling fan in the ceiling; guaranteed to put back some of the pounds lost on endless patrols. Particularly welcome were Malay curries with curried vegetables and a colourful variety of mouth-watering side-dishes.

Being a little larger in numbers, the Sergeants entertained more frequently. With a visit from a local Police Office or planter and his wife as the excuse, available Officers were always invited to share in the hottest of curries – curries that any self-respecting Indian would have considered a travesty of the real thing and certainly inedible. The highlight of the festivity would be a casual invitation to a gullible newly-joined Officer to eat one of the 'local delicacies', a raw chilli. The resulting exruciating searing pain on the lips and in the mouth, which no amount of lager could quickly alleviate, inevitably provided the Sergeants with considerable amusement. Byrne still winced as he remembered this most painful of experiences.

'Corporals and below' also had their entertainment, though as the Officers and Sergeants, in respect of women, they led by and large a monastic existence. Apart from infrequent trips to a local watering place, where they could enjoy a change of beer and food, Christmas and the Regimental Day provided the two main parties of the year. The former required turkey and Christmas pudding to be eaten at the hottest time of day and in keeping with long-standing Army traditions, the troops were waited upon with great care and attention and with much exchange of ribald pleasantries, by the Officers and Senior Ranks of the Company. The Regimental Day was in celebration of a famous Battle Honour won by the Regiment long ago. The celebrations were similar to Christmas only everyone had to sing for their supper in that all in Camp that day paraded in the morning to be inspected and addressed by the Battalion's Commanding Officer or Second-in-Command, as part of their whistle-stop tours. Difficult though it might be to understand by those far away and not immediately involved, there was always a spontaneous party in the canteen after a successful bandit kill. Though, if a few dollars were not retrieved, the Company and Platoon Commanders felt obliged to fund the festivities.

The Battalion occasionally held Regimental Guest Nights to which it was obligatory for the outlying Companies to send representatives. As all Officers in the Battalion got charged their share of the expense on their Mess bills, there was no disincentive for an impecunious National Service Second Lieutenant to attend. The chief guest was sometimes the Sultan of the State in which the Battalion was based, together with senior Civil Servants. As junior subaltern, Byrne was twice detailed to report for duty. They were magnificent occasions. The Officers were respendent in white mess jackets, bright cummerbunds, blue 'Number Two' dress trousers with the two thin red stripes down their sides denoting an infantry regiment. In candle light, the Regimental Silver was much admired, the band played the Regimental March and the marches of the military guests. Port,

Madeira and cigars circulated freely. Byrne concluded peacetime soldiering could have its attractions.

Regimental functions were not solely confined to the Officers' Mess. From time to time the R.S.M. decided his Mess needed to make its mark on the social calendar with a dinner or ball. The attendance of Company Sergeant Majors was required together with at least one Sergeant. The Mess always extended an invitation for at least one Officer from each Company to be present. Byrne found himself, again as the junior subaltern, detailed to attend one of these occasions – a ball. Not having a wife and not being acquainted with any local young ladies, he was able to concentrate his attentions totally on the finer points of etiquette surrounding a junior officer's behaviour at a Warrant Officers' and Sergeants' Mess Ball. Several wives had accompanied their husbands to Malaya. As the Battalion was almost entirely comprised in the junior ranks of National Servicemen, the wives in Malaya were those of the more senior Officers and Sergeants. Byrne sat at the Company table with the C.S.M., the C.Q.M.S. and their wives, together with two other C Company Sergeants. Dinner had been served, the remnants cleared away and the Dance Section of the Regimental Band was in splendid form. Byrne was well aware of his first duty, to dance with the Sergeant Major's wife. There was no shortage of small talk and dance after dance passed by without Byrne finding an opportunity to issue his invitation; a task made no easier by the necessity of his selecting a dance about which he had a working knowledge of the steps. There was a lull in the conversation and Byrne seized his chance. His request was both graciously received and accepted. Byrne triumphantly led Mrs. Sergeant Major on to the floor, passing the R.S.M. and Commanding Officer's table on his way; a triumph to be short-lived as the music stopped just as he was about to lead his partner off in a valeta. They clapped the band and Byrne extracted a promise for a further early opportunity to exhibit his terpsichorean talent. The animated small talk resumed. Once again Byrne anxiously waited for his opportunity. It came. Once more the music stopped as they reached the floor. Once more they clapped the band and resumed their seats. By now Byrne was beginning to perspire slightly with embarrassment and he decided it was time to take swift and decisive action, regardless of small talk or what dance the band was playing. As soon as the music started once more, he politely but firmly interrupted the conversation and a much-relieved Byrne and the Sergeant Major's wife managed to dance a just passable Quick Step. Byrne thanked his partner, took a long draught of wine and inwardly congratulated himself on a job well done. His self-esteem was quickly deflated. The Adjutant came over and indicated he wished to have a private word with him. It appeared he was the bearer of a personal message from the Commanding Officer, who 'would be much obliged if Mr. Byrne would stop dancing with the Sergeant Major's wife'. Byrne realised explanations at that time and place would be too long and involved. He subsided into his seat, inwardly seething that his earnest efforts to fulfil his duties as an Officer could be so cruelly misconstrued.

A signal arrived ordering that C Company's soccer team was to travel to Battalion Headquarters the following day to compete in the annual inter-Company competition. Even though there was only 8 Platoon in Camp, just having returned from an arduous but uneventful long patrol, the Company Commander said honour was at stake. No Yorkshire Fusilier Company had ever failed to enter the Football Competition and C Company was not going to be the first. Company Headquarters and 8 Platoon would therefore have to find the Company team. 8 Platoon were delighted. They considered themselves the best footballers anyway and Byrne was not surprised to see tired limbs forgotten as the hopefuls of the Platoon, with a handful from Company Headquarters, chased a ball around the tents in the stultifying heat of the afternoon sun. Wherever in the world the British soldier finds himself, if he has a ball and a few square yards, he will play football.

Byrne found himself in the team. This was certainly not in recognition of any particular footballing skill. Corporal Grice, the team Captain, explained with typical Yorkshire bluntness, that the Company's only goalkeeper was on patrol. Gingell, the water-truck driver, had enthusiastically volunteered but he was hopeless and the team had unanimously vetoed his inclusion. Mr. Byrne played rugby and should be fit, would he mind obliging? In any case, anyone would be better than Gingell. Byrne knew that in the unwritten rules for young subalterns there could, in the end, only be one answer to the request. In vain and in genuine modesty, he pleaded his lack of experience. He had played fullback once or twice but not very well, surely there must be someone else? Byrne secretly felt a little smug that clearly his men had identified him as some sort of sportsman, even though the comparison with the water-truck driver was hardly flattering. His ego was subsequently deflated when he learnt that a young rotund Regular Ordnance Company Officer, who had just joined the Company for a few weeks experience in the field, had previously been approached and had refused, pleading a prior engagement in the shape of urgent recces.

On Saturday morning, in their best uniforms, C Company's team got onto two flat trucks, rifles in one hand and footballing kit in the other. Escorted by the Scout Car they made their way the twenty miles to Battalion H.Q.

The first match was uneventful as far as Byrne was concerned. C Company were fortunate to have two young budding professionals in the forward line and two large full backs of little footballing ability but with the useful attribute of being able to deposit the ball, together with the wingers, over the touchline whenever the opposition ventured into the Company's half. Byrne had little to do but deal with the odd back pass, lean against a goalpost and take a mild interest in the proceedings in front of him. He naturally felt rather virtuous at his, albeit reluctant, participation in his soldiers' sporting activities.

Inevitably the Commanding Officer and Adjutant were present. The former to present the Cup, make encouraging noises about sportsmanship and say 'well played' at appropriate intervals; the latter to keep his eye on the proceedings in general to ensure there was no slippage of Regimental standards. In most Battalions if there was a choice, it was preferable for a young Officer to incur the wrath of the Commanding Officer, rather then the Adjutant. As is well-known, Adjutants are immaculately turned out, have an innate and pronounced sense of their own superiority and feel it is their duty to chastise subalterns, Second Lieutenants in particular, for real or imagined misdemeanours. It was just possible the Adjutant had a sense of humour or that he decided Byrne required his invaluable guidance. Passing behind the back of Byrne's goal on his stately perambulation, he remarked that, in his considered and though unsaid, obviously authoritative view, that goalkeeper was not the position in which he would expect to find an active young Officer. Byrne's mortification was complete.

There were other sporting moments. Byrne recalled the cricket match when Sergeant Lennox, who, surprisingly for a Scot, was convinced he was a slow bowler of some subtlety and was carted all over the field by the batsmen of a cavalry regiment. He remembered the somewhat subsequent strained relations on the next patrol, having taken him off after two overs. There was an embarrassing match on the padang against a team from the local village captained by the Chinese Postmaster who was second to none in his loyalty to King and Empire. He had recruited another ten less than enthusiastic Chinese whose knowledge of cricket was minimal. Byrne declared the Company's scratch side's innings closed at 300 for two wickets and had to instruct his bowlers to bowl slowly and away from the wicket to allow the opposition to reach double figures. He remembered the ability of tiny Chinese and Malay youngsters to return a badminton shuttle, no matter how hard it had been struck or well-directed from anywhere on the court and the tenacity of the students of the local school who, though diminutive, flung themselves kamikaze-fashion at the knees of the Battalion's Rugby team, making progress like walking through deep water.

Chapter 10

Food Galore

Byrne lay in his basha that night and still felt fragile. The Platoon had set off early that morning on the start of an unusual two-day patrol in an area of the jungle C Company had not previously explored. He lay on part of his poncho, gazed at the rest of it stretched a few inches above his head and regretted his over-indulgence the previous night. The visit of the Officers to the Sergeants' Mess had been a great social success and the Sergeants had been at their most hospitable. He now had three regrets, the late hour he had stayed, the amount of over-seasoned curry he had eaten and more especially, the quantity of Beck's beer he had drunk. The following morning, in reality only three hot and restless hours later, for the second and last time in Malaya, he had woken with a splitting headache. 8 Platoon seemed to him to be unnecessarily noisy and cheerful that morning as Sergeant Lennox checked their kit and weapons. A bumpy ride on the flat trucks up a jungle track had not improved his sense of well-being. Fortunately, the rest of the day's exertions had not been too strenuous. There had been no sign of bandits, their camps or any other living creature. He had carefully kept to those areas of the map where the contour lines were the farthest apart and so avoided the exertion of clambering up and down the steepest hillsides. As the day wore on he had felt somewhat better but now, in spite of the comparative cool of the night, his headache had returned and he was sick and hot. He looked at his luminous Army-issue wristwatch, it was 2.00 a.m. Three times already since turning-in he had picked up his carbine and armed himself with a plentiful supply of Army Form Blank before squatting down on the primitive latrine dug in the ground behind a tree, hanging on for support to a branch. Byrne was acutely conscious of the intense amusement of the sentries at the unusual and free entertainment their Platoon Commander

86

was providing to while away the night hours. Definitely not amusing to Byrne was the attention the mosquitoes paid to his bare bottom as nature took its course. The only thing for which he was thankful was that he was able to exclude the whining menaces when he returned to his basha.

What was unusual about the patrol was that with the Platoon was Ah Wong, a bandit who had surrendered to the Police some weeks before. Already, the Company Commander had said, shortly after his surrender, he had led A Company to two bandit camps. 3 Platoon had attacked the first, killed a sentry and in the resulting confusion as the bandits scattered into the jungle, the 'stops', small ambushes on likely lines of retreat, had wounded at least two more. The second camp was empty. The tame bandit had now been passed over to D Company, in whose area he claimed he knew of two more camps. He was right. The two large and spacious camps were found on rising ground, many miles in the depths of the jungle and not many yards away from small streams. When D Company's Platoons cautiously made their way into the camps from the surrounding jungle it was obvious they had been empty for several days. The news of Ah Wong's defection had clearly spread. He said he knew the whereabouts of at least one more camp, this time in C Company's area.

By this time, it was a virtual certainty that there was no chance of finding this camp occupied but it had to be investigated. Just in case, the Company Commander decided that 8 Platoon would approach the camp through the jungle from the rear and not risk raising the alarm by travelling through the local kampongs. Hence the long circuitous route on which 8 Platoon found themselves. In addition, it was many weeks since the Company had asked the Air Force for support. C Company should keep its name on the map at Brigade Headquarters. He had therefore requested an air strike on the camp area pointed out by the bandit in order to impress the local population.

Byrne felt better the following morning after stand-to and well enough to tackle several tinned soya sausages and mess tins of tea with a gusto, stemming from a stomach that had been thoroughly emptied during the previous night. Tins buried and weapons cleaned and checked, the Platoon was ready for the off. Ah Wong listened carefully as Byrne held his briefing, not understanding a word. In order that Byrne could communicate with him, a Chinese Policeman had been seconded to C Company. The bandit was obviously anxious to please. 8 Platoon viewed him with deep suspicion and the young Policeman treated him with positive disdain. Corporal Grice had volunteered to be the bandit's keeper. Byrne was quite sure Grice's devotion to duty lay more in his hope that the bandit would make a run for it than in wanting to be helpful. There was little chance of Ah Wong making a run for it, he thought. The more the ex-bandit sensed the hostility around him, the more keen he appeared to make himself amenable. The interpreter said Ah Wong was totally uncon-cerned that he was already responsible for the death of one and the wounding of two of his erstwhile comrades and appeared to be looking forward to the rewards that would result from his betrayals. Briefing over, the Platoon moved off.

The Platoon's start-line was halfway up a hillside from which they could see for several miles across an uninhabited area of jungle and patches of scrub and grassland. In the far distance, Byrne could just make out the bright blue of the Straits of Malacca. It was a gloriously clear morning. Ah Wong pointed out the location of the bandit camp which Byrne checked on his map. He noted with relief that it coincided with the reference given to the RAF. The bandit camp was rather more than a mile in front of them, in an area of jungle about a mile square. The air strike had been laid on for midday. It was then only mid-morning, so the Platoon settled down to wait. Sergeant Lennox was the only one who had seen a large-scale air strike before and he described, with that graphic detail of which only an older regular soldier is capable, the ferocity of the bombing and the accuracy of the rocket-firing Typhoons that could be expected. Sitting in the midst of his Platoon, admiring the panoramic view, sucking a boiled sweet from a tin Private Rice had opened and tingling with antici-pation, Byrne felt as though he was in the front seat of a cinema balcony.

The hours passed and punctually at 11.45 a.m. the air strike arrived. It was not in the form so vividly described by the Platoon Sergeant. Slowly over the horizon droned a majestic Sunderland Flying Boat. The huge white plane circled the target area in a dignified manner and promptly at midday, a number of what appeared to be small round black objects tumbled down. They exploded with disappointingly innocuous bangs among the trees below. When 8 Platoon returned to base the following day, the Company Commander apologised for the lack of overwhelming support and explained that there had been many calls for air strikes. The Platoon's operation had not warranted a high priority.

At the time, 8 Platoon had mixed emotions. Disappointment and hilarity fought for the upper hand. They put on their packs and filed down the hill. Using their normal formation through jungle, they fanned out into an arrowhead pattern as they crossed more open spaces. After about half a mile they came across a stream. The bandit signalled that the position of the bandit camp was upstream in the jungle and not far ahead. A narrow track ran alongside the water on the right. The Platoon moved cautiously up both sides of the stream with six men in front in extended line. Byrne, put himself in the centre, walking by the stream. He told Ah Wong to give him plenty of warning before they reached the camp and kept him close behind him.

The ex-bandit had lost his bearings or didn't know the area well. Byrne received no warning. The left-hand bank gradually rose as the Platoon moved quietly forward. The track bent sharply down to the stream and then up the other bank. At this point the leading members of the Platoon almost walked into the bandit camp without realising it. It was a large area, cleared of undergrowth among the trees, with steps down to the stream cut into the steep bank. Though they didn't know for certain at the time, the bandits had fled and the camp was empty. With safety catches off and nerves on edge, the Platoon moved quietly through the deserted camp. The sinking feeling in the pit of Byrne's stomach slowly faded as he realised the bandit camp was unoccupied and no shots would be coming from the surrounding jungle. Ah Wong was outwardly totally relaxed. He, at least, seemed totally convinced that there were none of his old companions anywhere near. No doubt this lack of concern stemmed from a belief all along that he was likely to be leading 8 Platoon to an unoccupied camp.

The camp did show obvious signs of fairly recent occupation and probably a hurried but not panic-stricken evacuation. There were a few tins lying around with tiny scraps of food in them. These almost indiscernible remnants were still being attacked by ants. The area was littered with bits of dry paper which had not yet degenerated into a soggy mess. It was not a large camp. Byrne and Sergeant Lennox estimated from the remains of a few bashas and flattened areas, where there had been tents of some sort, that it had housed ten to fifteen men and women at most. There was a small hospital. Two rickety shelters had old camp beds inside with a few discarded bandages on the ground, on some of which there were fading patches of blood. A thorough search of the camp revealed no documents, no weapons and nothing much of interest. Byrne was disappointed but he had expected little else. They did find two positions which had been used by sentries. One was twenty yards down the track by which they had approached the camp and only a few feet off it. No one had spotted the position during the advance. The Platoon realised the implications and thanked their lucky stars the camp had been unoccupied.

There was one item in the camp of intense interest; a medium-sized enamelled hip bath. They marvelled as to how such a bulky and heavy object could have been brought to the camp. The nearest village was several miles away. Ah Wong was unable to enlighten them.

The Platoon set up its own base alongside the old bandit camp. While they were doing this the ex-bandit engaged in animated conversation with the Police interpreter. It appeared that Ah Wong had just remembered that he had heard, a long time ago, that there was a food dump nearby. He did not know exactly where it was but thought it might be to the east of the camp, only a few hundred yards away. With nothing better to do while the Platoon brewed up and used their ponchos to erect bashas, Byrne and five men set off in the direction indicated by Ah Wong. After a few minutes, they came across a large open space on a gently sloping hillside, dotted with several clumps of bushes. From the expression on Ah Wong's face, he could help no further as to the food dump's location, if it existed. As they passed the first of the bushes, it was Batman Rice who noticed six large gleaming tins dug part way into the ground and tucked into the undergrowth round the base of the greenery. The tins would have been invisible to the casual passerby and the bandits could bank on the chances of them being found under normal circumstances as nil. The men scattered and looked round the bases of the other bushes on the slope. Under nearly every bush there were more tins, scores of tins, dug into shallow pits. There were tins of pilchards, condensed milk and dozens of large kerosine tins of rice. There were tins of food of all kinds. Byrne sent for more of his men to help get the cache together. It took half the Platoon nearly an hour to search the whole area and get all the tins in one place. It was an enormous treasure trove of food. The soldiers looked at the mountain of food in awe, none of them had seen anything like it before. It was no wonder that the bandits had neither the manpower nor the time to move it after they had heard of the defection of Ah Wong. Byrne debated whether it would be worth laying an ambush and hope for the bandits' return to collect what must have been supplies for many months for most of the bandits in the State. He decided against it as it might be many weeks before they returned, even if they did not decide to write off the dump as a grievous loss. The ponderous presence and bombing by the Sunderland would have told them that the camp, at least, was known to the Security Forces.

There was no question of 8 Platoon trying to move the food back to their base and he knew the Company Commander would be hardly likely to deploy the whole Company on such an exercise. Byrne gave the order and they set to work with a will with their bayonets, to pierce all the tins and spread the contents on the ground. The humid heat and insects would render the food unusable within hours. This mass destruction did not start until Sergeant Lennox had appropriated some of the tins of rice and condensed milk for his own use.

Back in the bandit camp, Sergeant Lennox ordered that the hip bath be taken down to the stream and given a thorough clean. That evening he announced his intention of making the biggest rice pudding ever seen in Malaya. Whether it was the biggest rice pudding could have been a matter for argument but the Platoon satiated themselves on what was certainly the richest.

During the night the unexpected happened. In the early hours a sentry thought he heard some rustling in the distance. The Platoon was quietly brought to stand-to and they all listened. The rustling came nearer and from perhaps the distance of a cricket pitch away, a somewhat plaintive voice called, 'Lim.' Byrne whispered to the Police interpreter to tell the intruder that everything was all right and he should come into the camp. This he did and the Platoon waited, weapons cocked. Whether the invitation was unconvincing or not the one expected will never be known. After a few minutes of silence, Byrne led a small section of men in the direction from which the voice had come. They stopped frequently to listen but they could hear nothing other than the usual night-time chirruping and whirring noises of the jungle. They were on a narrow track which eventually led to much more open scrubland. From a small knoll they were able to see far into the distance. It was a beautiful tropical night and bright moonlight turned the ground in front into a patchwork of dark shadows and what seemed to be patches of still water where the light was reflected from the smooth grass. They waited for an hour but saw nothing. The intruder was either behind them, sheltering in the jungle, or somewhere out there, crouched in the shadows.

The Platoon was disappointed. A contact of any kind was rare and should not be missed. There was little doubt the intruder, or intruders, was a member of the Min Yuen from one of the villages some distance away. He certainly hadn't known the camp had been abandoned and may even have been hoping to win comradely approval for reporting that an Army patrol was in the area. Byrne only hoped the shock he must have received had been sufficient to make one badly scared Chinese Communist mend his ways.

Though Byrne could not claim any credit, C Company and 8 Platoon in particular, for a short while basked in the success of the destruction of the large food dump. Surprisingly, as such finds were rare, it was only a few days later that food dumps were the topic of conversation in 8 Platoon once again. The local Police Inspector said that he had been told that there was a food dump hidden in the bank of the river above the village of Batu Gajah. More than this he had been unable to find out and his informant had only heard this from another, who in turn had heard it from someone else and so on. Instead of a day off, the Company Commander suggested that Byrne and his Platoon should investigate. The discovery of the previous week could have been the start of a winning streak? In any case, the day off they were due for could always be taken at some future date? Byrne and Sergeant Lennox were outwardly enthusiastic at the idea. The remainder of the Platoon were less so, having anticipated a welcome change of beer and food. An examination of the map robbed both the Platoon Commander and Sergeant of most of any enthusiasm. The river in question ran, according to the map, for at least eight miles above the village and probably for a lot farther before the source.

It was pouring down with rain when they mounted the flat trucks the following morning. The rain was positively torrential as they debussed at the village and squelched their way through the mud round the encircling wire fence and looked at the dirty swollen waters of the river. The river was not broad, which made searching of the far bank easier than it might otherwise have been. Even so, every now and again, it was necessary for a member of the Platoon to wade across the river up to his chest in water to check on an overgrown part of the far bank or a mass of brushwood behind which something could have been concealed. After the first few hundred yards, every man was so thoroughly soaked by the rain, or immersion in the swirling waters, that any thoughts of trying to keep dry were completely forgotten.

The Platoon followed a narrow well-used track by the river. Sometimes it ran close by the water, where the bank was so low that nothing could be concealed and examination of the rising ground above the track was easy. In other places, the track ran along the top of a high bank that sloped almost vertically down to the water. Brockley, Hird and Rice swore as they scrambled across the muddy slippery surfaces, hanging on to the protruding roots of trees and trying to avoid involuntary submersion in the uninviting water below. To make the searching of the banks easier, Byrne tried splitting the Platoon into two parties, one on each bank, but the undergrowth on the far bank was so thick that progress was painfully slow and the idea was quickly abandoned. They had searched for over a mile and a very wet, mud-covered 8 Platoon was prepared to call it a day. However, orders were orders and they persevered. Rice, as one of the lightest and smallest men in the patrol, more than once found himself protesting, upside down and suspended by his feet, being urged by the Platoon Sergeant to search the vertical stretches of the bank below. The track became even more narrow and less used. The rain did not lessen in intensity. Any self-respecting bandit would long ago have taken shelter.

After his efforts during the day, it was only fair that Rice should discover the cache. From an inverted position, his feet held firmly by Brockley and Hird, Rice found himself looking at a line of shiny tins, some large, some small. The bandits had excavated a twelve feet long, two feet deep shelf among the tree roots. Some twenty or more tins of the usual rice, condensed milk and fish were arranged neatly on two thin planks which, resting on more substantial roots, prevented any danger of the tins falling into the river below. Byrne guessed it was a halfway house between the local Min Yuen and the bandits. Though only a small fraction of the food dump they had discovered earlier in the month, the find made the patrol worthwhile. Particularly as, travelling light, the Platoon was able to bring the tins back triumphantly to camp. Care was taken to show the tins to the villagers on their way back with much shaking of heads and wagging of fingers. There was little doubt the supplies had come via some communist cell in the village. Though unlikely by itself to have any great effect on the State of Emergency, the discovery would certainly be an irritant, a source of food that would have to be replaced by another, probably more risky, supply. Getting the bandits to take more risks, however small, was one way of winning the war.

Chapter 11

Variety

There were unexpected repercussions following the destruction of the large food dump by 8 Platoon. The consequences could have been serious but in the event caused only some momentary alarm. Intelligence reports several weeks later were to the effect that the local M.R.L.A. Independent Platoon leader, who it appears had been the mastermind behind the dump, was greatly angered by its loss. Reading between the lines of the testimony of several informers, the collecting together of that amount of food had taken very many months of patient hard work. The bandits had understandably taken its destruction very much to heart. Their leader, undoubtedly hoping to add to his charisma, had publicly vowed vengeance on the soldiers who had perpetrated the deed and at the same time, reminded the local population of his own indestructibility by claiming that he could only be killed by a silver bullet. Clearly these bellicose claims were meant to encourage the local Chinese to flock to his colours. Under the prevailing circumstances in the State, where the bandits had recently taken several hard knocks, it was not surprising there were no signs of this happening and it was encouraging to both the Yorkshire Fusiliers and the Police that the loss of so much food had warranted such a display of outrage and had been a serious setback to the well-being of the bandits and to whatever plans the local bandits had.

It was 9 Platoon and not 8 that felt the bandit wrath. 9 Platoon was patrolling along the seashore of the Malacca Straits late one dark evening, only a few miles beyond the deserted camp that had been revealed to 8 Platoon by the bandit deserter. The jungle came right up to the beach. From the top of a high promontory at a distance of 200 yards, came ragged firing aimed in the general direction of 9 Platoon. The bandit firing was uncontrolled, high and mostly wide. Nevertheless, this was of no immediate comfort to 9 Platoon who sought whatever cover they could find in the dunes and jungle edges and fired a considerable amount of ammunition in swift reply in the general direction of where the muzzle flashes had been seen. The bandits didn't wait for very long after their initial burst of bravado. Either intentionally, or shaken by the ferocity of the response, they quickly disappeared. There were no dead or wounded bandits to be found when 9 Platoon searched the area and the Platoon had suffered no casualties, not even a near miss; though this did not detract from the war stories told in the canteen the following day. Possibly the leader of the M.R.L.A. Independent Platoon felt honour had been satisfied but that must have been his only satisfaction. It was unfortunately another Battalion that a year later shot him from ambush with a very ordinary .303 rifle bullet.

8 Platoon patrolled every day for week after monotonous week. Whether the patrol was an outing for one day or a ten-day marathon made no difference. There were bandits in the area but they either avoided contact or the Platoon was looking in the wrong places. The other two Platoons of C Company had no better luck. The apparent fruitlessness of their efforts and lack of excitement made even the most enthusiastic National Serviceman think rather more than before of the date on which he would board the plane in Singapore and fly back to the U.K. Meanwhile, any newly issued jungle green uniforms quickly faded in the hot sun and torrential downpours into a light shade of greenish-grey; purple patches under the arms and in the crotch, where patches of soreness had spread, were painfully treated and feet were examined daily to make sure they were not disintegrating.

After nearly a month of having nothing to report and the other Companies every now and again adding to the Battalion's score, the whole of C Company was cheered by the success of 7 Platoon. Unusually precise information was received early one afternoon, that there was to be a pickup of food the following morning. One bandit would be collecting it. The time of collection would be 11.00 a.m. Even the position of the tree on an open hillside, under which the food had already been hidden, was carefully pinpointed. The site was near the local village and little more than two miles from the Company's base. 7 Platoon was in camp and got the job. So detailed and inviting was the information that a possible bandit ambush of the ambushers was thought more than probable. However, such a tip-off could not be ignored.

7 Platoon Commander was able to do his reconnaissance in comfort. Along the bottom of the hillside in question ran a minor road, frequently

used by the Company's and Police vehicles. While being driven slowly past in a Land-Rover, the Platoon Commander and his escort, ostensibly taking no more than usual interest in the passing countryside, were able to locate the tree with ease. It stood prominently halfway down a fairly steep cleared slope thirty yards from the jungle which covered the top of the incline; the jungle from which the bandit was due to appear. In case of watching eyes, it was not possible to investigate further. There were a few small clumps of bushes dotted around the orange-brown stony hillside but no other cover. Certainly not enough to conceal twenty-five men.

The Platoon Commander decided he had to compensate for any bandit intention of a shoot-up of his Platoon with increased vigilance and he would take only four men. He would use two of the clumps of bushes as cover. The rest of 7 Platoon would wait by the trucks in Camp, ready to follow-up if necessary. The five men left on foot early enough to be in position before dawn.

The grey dawn found five men of 7 Platoon prone in the sparse grass, as deep as they could get into the shadows of two bushes which were twenty yards apart and no greater distance from the tree. They lay perfectly still, the whiteness of their faces concealed behind dark net veils, the backs of their hands smeared with mud so no telltale patches of white could be seen. It was impossible to check, even at such a close distance and in the clear light of day what, if anything, lay beneath the tree. They had not wasted time in examining the area during their cautious approach up the crumbling slope in the dark early hours of the morning.

Along the road below them, some early morning workers cycled their way towards the local estates and a lorry filled with vegetables and cages of clucking hens went by on the way to market. The temperature rose steadily as the hours passed. Even in the shadow of the bushes, the reflected heat from the light-coloured soil and rocks around them caused sweat to drip from their faces and dark patches of sweat stained their shirts. They did not dare reach for their waterbottles in case the movement would give them away to alert eyes watching from the jungle above. A lorry load of brown-clad Malay Special Constables passed by. They were in a very good mood, chattering, laughing and holding their rifles in an unmilitary way which would have been little use if they had run into an ambush. The Platoon Commander made a mental note to pass on his observations to the local Police Inspector. As the time moved towards 11.00 a.m. the five men watched the jungle edge, thirty-five yards away, more and more carefully. Eleven a.m. came and went. They tensed but nothing happened. They relaxed a little and the men wondered how long the Platoon Commander would decide to stay.

At twenty minutes past 11.00 a.m. the five men saw above them a lone khaki-clad figure standing against the green of the leaves behind him. His head was uncovered, his dark hair was long and he clutched a Lee Enfield Rifle tightly across his chest. He looked apprehensive and gazed at the road in front of him. So intent was he on the road that he appeared to give no more than a cursory glance at the clumps of bush that dotted the slope. Clearly his concern was being caught in the open by some passing military foot or vehicle patrol. 7 Platoon held its fire. Though the bandit was only thirty or forty yards from them, a miss would mean they would have little chance of catching him as he fled into the jungle behind. The bandit decided all was safe and rapidly slid and stumbled his way down to the tree, he bent over towards something on the ground. There was a short sharp burst of firing and he fell forward dead.

The kill, though a welcome addition to the Company's score, remained a mystery. The food the bandit was collecting was a small amount of rice. The cache was hardly worth the journey; unless the bandits really were feeling the pinch, or someone knew what was going to happen and was not going to waste a large amount of food to be recovered by the Army. This last thought and unusual accuracy of the tip-off was such that C Company speculated that someone, a disaffected local member of the Min Yuen or even, perhaps the bandit hierarchy, had decided for some reason to get rid of an unreliable or ineffective member of the Party. Maybe C Company had unwittingly been cast in the role of the executioner.

The next two weeks found 8 Platoon becoming a little bored. The other Platoons, for various reasons, particular knowledge of an area or availability at the time wanted, spent more time on patrol than it did. Hence 8 Platoon found itself with periods of two and even three days at a time on standby in camp. There was no question of extra nights in the seaside resort, there could be an emergency. Bandits might attack a train, a planter's bungalow, a bus or a police post. 8 Platoon was C Company's reserve. Life in camp was not exciting. The C.S.M. found time for morning parades and some drill. This was not popular. Weapons were cleaned, tested and inspected; more often than was necessary in the opinion of the Platoon. There were minor and not very exhausting fatigues but nevertheless, irritating interruptions to time that could be better spent dozing. The weather seemed to be more sticky and hot than usual. Night guard duty came round frequently. After letters had been written home, over a bottle of beer in the canteen the opinion was often expressed that they much preferred the jungle to the C.S.M. and guard duty in the tent by the gate. Byrne did his best but his organisation of impromptu games of football and housey-housey sessions began to pall. Byrne felt much the same as his Platoon. Though he was spared the delights of early morning drill, the supervising of lethargic soldiers was in itself tedious. It was almost a welcome break to get up in the middle of the night, dress and make sure the guard was in order. The main attraction to him of being in camp was an evening game of mah-jong and drinking bottles of cold lager under the slowly revolving fan in the ceiling.

Occasionally, when patrols were few and contacts with the bandits even fewer, there were some interesting, if not exciting interludes. C Company was detailed, on regular occasions, to provide a guard for the night express which ran from Singapore to Kuala Lumpur. The guard was required from the station in the nearby village to Seremban, a long stretch of railway where there had been occasional derailments and where, from time to time from the cover of the jungle, the bandits had used the passing train for target practice. The occasional wrecked item of rolling stock alongside the side of the track and holes in the carriages testified to their activities. For several months, nothing more serious than a few badly directed shots at the passing carriages had been reported but the danger was still there and chances were not being taken of anything more serious happening to a train often packed with civilians and troops. Byrne remembered the irregular line of bullet holes alongside his head when he travelled on the same upcountry train many months before.

None of C Company's three Platoons was up to strength but for this duty, as for most others, it did not matter. A half-platoon of twelve men was more than enought to guard the night express. Late in the evening, Byrne and half of 8 Platoon sat on the empty platform of the small railway station with only a minor railway official for company. The platform was empty because the express itself did not stop at such a minor wayside halt. However, at the appointed time and in the rapidly gathering darkness, a pilot engine pushing flat wagons steamed up and 8 Platoon climbed aboard. They adjusted the low parapet of sandbags that ran round the edge of the trucks. The small but powerful searchlight at the front of the wagon was manned. Bren guns were set up on either side and a 2 inch Mortar with parachute illuminating flares and high explosive bombs handy was placed in the middle of the truck. Byrne checked that he had with him his badge of office as commander of the small expedition, a Verey pistol and that he knew in which pockets he had put the red and green cartridges. The signals, if they were required, were clear. A red flare would stop the express and a green flare would allow it to set off again. The theory behind the use of the pilot train was equally straightforward. The pilot train was the stalking-horse. If there was something suspicious on the track revealed in the beam of the searchlight, Byrne would fire the red flare and investigate. Any such obstruction aimed at derailing or stopping the express, if the bandits knew their business, would be covered by fire, so it was worthwhile staying alert.

To offset any possible tedium, there were some compensations. On either side of the track, certain areas of jungle, well away from habitations, were designated as areas where there could be prophylactic fire. This meant that the Platoon could direct light machine gun and rifle fire into the jungle ahead of the truck. The idea was to discourage the bandits, at least in these places, from lying in wait to attack the train. How effective this stratagem was was difficult to assess but 8 Platoon enjoyed the diversion. Though precise aiming was neither called for nor possible, tracer ammunition was liberally distributed in the Bren gun and rifle magazines. When Byrne, studying his map in the light of a torch, gave the order, the effect was breathtaking as the bright lights curved into the trees ahead and 8 Platoon expended large quantities of ammunition with great enthusiasm.

Prophylactic fire had caused unexpected difficulties in the past. Telephone lines ran alongside the railway track. Every now and again communications had been lost. This had meant repair parties, with armed escorts, had been ordered out several times to repair the faults. At first, the telephone authorities believed that the damage to the ceramic insulators on the telegraph poles was sabotage by bandits, intent on causing minor irritation. The times when the faults occurred led to it being proved that this was not the case. Some riflemen, fancying themselves as sharpshooters, when the Platoon Commander was not looking, could not resist taking snap shots at the white pots as they loomed up before them in the searchlight's beam. Strict orders were issued to Pilot Train Commanders that this practice would cease forthwith; so depriving the conscripts of an enjoyable pastime.

One particular night's duty on the pilot train remained vividly in Byrne's memory. For some days a newly arrived Sergeant from the U.K. had accompanied 8 Platoon on its patrols. Destined to be shortly posted as a Platoon Sergeant to another Company, Sergeant Evans had been placed for two weeks under the guidance of Sergeant Lennox and Byrne. The two Sergeants had struck up an immediate friendship, not least because of a shared sense of humour that occasionally verged on the mischievous.

Naturally, when 8 Platoon had been detailed for railway duty, Sergeant Evans had volunteered to go along as part of his education.

With two Sergeants aboard, Byrne felt even more relaxed than usual about taking a ten minutes nap and handing over command to Sergeant Lennox. He settled down on the floor of the wagon, laid his head on a spare sandbag and dozed off. Still in a state of semi-consciousness he heard the two Sergeants discussing, in slow and leisured tones, what was clearly a matter of concern but not apparently of any great urgency.

Evans: 'Is this a matter we should draw to the attention of the Platoon Commander?'
Lennox: 'Or should we fire the red flare ourselves?'
Evans: 'We could wake the Officer and ask him for his advice?'
Lennox: 'The matter certainly needs thought. However, taking into account all the circumstances, I think we should take the responsibility ourselves and fire the flare.'
Evans: 'I agree, let us ask Mr. Byrne for the pistol.'

From half-heard snatches of this disturbing conversation and as his mind cleared, Byrne grasped the essential message that there was something ahead which might require a red flare. Alarmed, he sat bolt upright in time to see, shining white in the beam of the searchlight, the unopened gates of a level crossing across the track only a few yards in front. The flat truck hit the gates and there were two sharp cracks as they snapped off and flew into the surrounding darkness.

The pilot engine had already started to slow down. Byrne fired a red flare and the night train stopped. He walked back to make sure there was nothing on the line that might cause a problem for the following train. There were only a few tiny slivers of wood scattered over the shining rails and around the crossing. There was also a panic-stricken Indian crossing keeper who appeared from the small hut alongside the track. He apologised loudly and at length for having failed to open the level crossing gates at the appointed time. Byrne realised that he, too, must have been asleep. Momentarily he felt sorry for the distraught crossing keeper, anticipating the coals of fire that undoubtedly would be heaped on his luckless head the following morning. As it was well after curfew and there would be no traffic, nothing more needed to be done. Byrne walked back to his delighted Platoon, fired a green flare and the pilot engine and the night express resumed their journeys. The Sergeants vigorously protested their innocence and blamed the short time available after they had seen the closed crossing gates for their lack of action. Byrne knew better.

The welcome coolness of the breeze on the night train ride and the opportunity to warm the barrels of the Platoon's armoury were always followed by the anticlimax. Having finished their guard duty the Platoon lay, dozing fitfully, on the hard benches of the comfortless waiting room on Seremban station, fortified only by the tasteless cheese sandwiches the cooks had prepared. The local early morning train returned them to their duties.

Cheese sandwiches were not popular and food was always of interest to 8 Platoon. In spite of the traditional banter between the soldiery and the Company Cooks, food in camp was passable and reasonably fresh. When on patrol, though few would admit it, the 'compo' rations weren't considered too bad either. Tinned soya link sausages for breakfast were boring after several days but the evening meal was always eagerly anticipated. Under the personal supervision of Sergeant Lennox, the required tins were collected from the packs and the result was a savoury 'all-in' stew. The routine and the quality never varied.

The bandits were always anxious to create an impression of strength to overawe the local population. Opportunities to sneak into villages to pressurise the inhabitants became fewer as the policy of enclosing the kampongs with wire fencing was pushed ahead. The wire fences made it far more difficult to the Min Yuen to sneak out food as they had to pass the sentries at the gates who would investigate any package that seemed suspicious. Perhaps as a consequence of this and also to remind everyone the M.R.L.A. were still a power in the land, the bandits indulged in a spate of stopping buses, confiscating any food, giving the passengers a lecture on the delights of Communism and then burning the bus. After the third bus in as many weeks was burnt in the Company area, the Company Commander decided it was time to call a halt. Though it seemed reasonable to assume that these interrupted journeys and enforced contributions from the public to the local bandits were not having the result of winning the hearts and minds of the population the bandits expected, particularly those of the bus passengers, it was time to stop, or at least discourage such lawless practices.

The obvious was done. The Company's Scout Car followed some buses, either at a discreet distance behind or showing the flag immediately in front. Occasionally the Cavalry joined in the fun and when they could be spared, the three Platoons provided truck-mounted sections for this duty. Several weeks passed and their efforts seemed to be having the desired effect. Much petrol was being used and the soldiers saw a great deal of the countryside but the bus burnings stopped. Unfortunately, there were very many bus journeys and nowhere near enough troops to spare to police more than a fraction of the total. After three weeks, in the middle of a lonely stretch of road with long clear views in both directions, an unguarded bus was stopped, the passengers were given a brief lecture on the fight for freedom and the bus was burnt.

A new approach was needed. Early one morning, six men of 8 Platoon stepped out of the jungle, where they had been dropped off some hours before, flagged down a bus and boarded it. Armed with Owen and Sten guns, they laid on the floor out of sight, near the entrance and emergency exits. The floor of the bus was not very clean, they anticipated they would be bitten by numerous insects and their fears proved correct. The journey to the next village was uneventful and uncomfortable. The concern of the passengers *en route* was manifest. They clearly thought the soldiers knew the bus was going to be attacked and had no desire to be in the middle of a small battle. Two days later, on the other side of the State, 7 Platoon did the same thing and again a week later. There were no kills and no contacts but the bandits' Intelligence sources worked quickly. No longer could the bandits stop an apparently unescorted bus with confidence. This finally put a stop to bus burnings. No more were burnt in C Company's area, much to the relief of the bus companies.

Though Byrne occasionally met local dignitaries in the course of his duties, the Emergency tended to make social contacts between the soldier and the ordinary Malay or Chinese infrequent. However, from observation and occasional conversations with those they met on patrol, it was obvious there was little rapport between the two races. The Chinese tended to be generally busy and to own more of the businesses and shops than would be expected from the proportion they formed of the population. Many Malays seemed to show little interest in material success, be it in manufacturing or commerce. They were a handsome race, particularly the women, thought 8 Platoon, with an innate sense of superiority which extended to the Chinese and in Byrne's view, probably to most Europeans as well! They were an eminently likeable, happy people with few of their number in the jungle. It was, however, the considered opinion of 8 Platoon, setting aside the major companies' rubber estates, the more unkempt a small estate was, the more likely it was to be owned by a Malay. After the Singapore riots, Byrne wondered if there could ever be an entirely untroubled future for the country.

He remembered the Platoon checking an isolated hut on the edge of a village. Living there, most unusually, were a young Chinaman and his

Malay wife. They offered him a sickly-sweet cup of thick black coffee. They were anxious to talk and Byrne felt flattered. From them he learnt, that no-one, Chinese or Malay, had spoken to them since their marriage several years before. Byrne wondered how they could even have met and didn't envy the years of lonely existence ahead of them.

The local planters were always friendly and welcomed visits whether they were social or if 8 Platoon showed the flag on their estate. The nearest planter's bungalow was less than four miles away to the east of the Com-pany's base. Late one evening the sound of shots came from that direction. There was no answer to an urgent telephone call from the Company Commander. 8 Platoon was scrambled. As the likely military response to such a situation was entirely predictable, even to the most amateurish bandit, the Platoon kept a wary eye open for trouble as they drove along the gloomy laterite roads; though it would have been brave bandits to have the effrontery to set an ambush among the serried ranks of rubber trees in the middle of a well-groomed large estate which afforded little cover.

The Platoon's trucks swept through the open gates in the tall perimeter barbed wire fence round the bungalow. An agitated Malay Special Consta-ble waved them through. From the excited N.C.O. standing in front of the bungalow, Byrne learnt that the Tuan was away for the night and that there had just been a burst of firing from the trees which had hit the bungalow. The N.C.O. pointed out holes in the woodwork. 'From where exactly had the shots come?' The N.C.O. waved his rifle vaguely in the direction of a long section of the fence. By now it was quite dark. Byrne decided there was little that could be done under the circumstances. The bandits could be anywhere by now. To at least discourage any further inci-dents that night, the Platoon, nothing loath, fired several volleys and bursts of L.M.G. fire in the general direction indicated by the Malay Corporal.

The following morning Byrne and Sergeant Lennox revisited the scene. They examined the bullet holes in the bungalow and then walked to that part of the perimeter wire from where the shots appeared to have come. They could see where the Platoon's firing had punctured bleeding holes in the rubber trees. Sergeant Lennox found the small pile of newly-fired cartridge cases of .303 ammunition just inside the fence. The Special Constables had said they had not fired back. In any case, even if they had, they certainly would not have been so brave or foolhardy to rush towards bandits just outside the wire in order to do so and the bullet cases would not have been in a pile. The Special Constables had fired at their own bungalow.

Byrne and Lennox could see what had happened but they did not understand why, though clearly an offence of some kind had been committed. They went to see the local Police Inspector who was not pleased. The next day he had the full story. The Special Constables were suffering from an acute combination of fear, loneliness and a desire to be nearer the fleshpots of the town; with the last-mentioned probably the most prominent in their minds. In their naivety, by firing at the bungalow they were paid to defend, they hoped to convince their superiors that the bungalow was too isolated, too dangerous to guard and that it should be evacuated

Such behaviour was not typical. No-one could really envy the lot of the Special Constables in their black berets, belts and khaki uniforms, being bounced around in the back of a Land-Rover while the planter did his rounds – never sure it wasn't their turn to be ambushed.

Chapter 12

Mixed Fortunes

Byrne sometimes remembered with nostalgia when he was a small boy and fished off the end of the pier with a handline at Whitby and the pride with which he would take home the very occasional, small codling for his Grandmother to cook. He also remembered, with considerably less enthusiasm, fishing from a small boat off Whitby, in miserable weather, with his Father and being desperately seasick. A belief that the movement of the sea and his sense of balance were incompatible had been reinforced, though this had not been necessary, by the agonising voyage across the Bay of Biscay. When the local Indian Police Inspector proposed a fishing trip, on a mutual day-off, in the Straits of Malacca, it was not surprising Byrne received the invitation with mixed feelings. He was asked to bring along hand grenades, which he was told were essential. This was a sufficiently intriguing request for him to accept. Had not the Company Commander stressed the importance of always maintaining good relationships with the civilian authorities and the Police?

The Police Inspector owned a small boat and outboard motor which he kept in a hut by a large bay. Byrne obtained twenty-four hand grenades for grenade throwing practice by 8 Platoon from a disbelieving C.Q.M.S. Armed with his carbine, the grenades in a sack, the detonators nestling against his cheese sandwiches and bottles of beer, Byrne was ready. Accompanied by two armed policemen, the Inspector drove the small party in his Land-Rover to the beach.

Byrne noted with relief that the sea was flat calm. In the middle of the bay was a large rusting hulk. This was all that remained of a Japanese merchant ship carrying troops south from Burma during the last days of W.W.II. It had been attacked by submarine, badly damaged and beached. The Inspector said that it was well known locally that many fish were to be found nearby.

They slowly circled the wreck and dropped grenades into the water at intervals. Byrne had secretly hoped for shoals of fish to take back triumphantly to provide a welcome change of diet for C Company. He was disappointed. Explosion after underwater explosion failed to produce anything more than one small fish, a fish even smaller than the codling Byrne had caught off Whitby pier. In the distance a few larger fish leapt out of the water in protest. Grenades exhausted, Byrne and the Inspector lay back in the sunshine, drank beer and reminisced. While the Inspector dozed, Byrne settled back in the bows of the boat and contemplated the events of the last week. It had been a hectic seven days.

The previous Sunday, Byrne had decided to show the flag personally around the local large rubber estates. It was a waste of manpower and boring for platoons, or even sections, to tramp round mile after mile of laterite roads and rubber trees without something tangible in view. However, planters and when they were married, their wives, welcomed courtesy calls from the Army. Social life for them was limited, for obvious reasons, to occasional escorted visits to the nearest club, which could be very many miles away and mutual invitations to Sunday tiffin or dinner to the manager of the estate next door. A further incentive to Byrne was the certainty of several free cold beers and the strong possibility of one or two invitations to Malayan or Indian curries over the coming weeks.

The usual Humber Scout Car driver was away driving something else on a detail to Battalion Headquarters. Most of the other drivers were also away, picking up or setting down 7 and 9 Platoons. Hearing of the impending outing, Private Gingell, the water-truck driver, enthusiastically volunteered his services. He confessed he had never driven the Scout Car before, or any other armoured vehicle for that matter. However, to drive the Scout Car was a long-cherished ambition and it would be a welcome and glamorous change from his usual lumbering water truck. There were one or two versatile and competent drivers available but for once, Byrne hadn't the heart to rebuff Gingell's heartfelt eagerness to help. Against his own better judgement and very much against that of the M.T. Corporal, Byrne agreed.

Byrne left Camp, sat behind twin-mounted Bren guns, in his second-best uniform, driven by a proud Gingell in his best. A missed gear and a jolt as he turned right onto the main road caused the M.T. Corporal to raise his eyes heavenwards. Gingell, having finally got the vehicle into top gear on a straight stretch of road, kept the Scout Car smoothly rolling along at thirty m.p.h.; Byrne relaxed.

The first call was only three miles away. On Byrne's instruction,

Gingell turned left onto a wide laterite road which led to the bungalow of the manager of the Jeram Padang Estate. The road ran straight for 100 yards, then there was a bend to the right. It was broad daylight and it was a very slight bend. Gingell was driving slowly and carefully at no more than twenty-five m.p.h. and there seemed to be no apparent reason why he should ignore the bend and drive straight into a small swamp. There was, of course, a difference between the panoramic view from the elevated seat of a water truck and peering through the driver's slit in front of the much lower seat of the Scout Car. Whatever the reason, which was never established, the vehicle was well and truly stuck. The indignity of sitting in the top hatch of a Scout Car, which was already down to axles in mud, was not lost on either Byrne or a crestfallen Gingell.

After the Scout Car had sunk fairly quickly to the level of the top of the wheels, a descent which caused Gingell to vacate his low-lying seat with alacrity, Byrne managed to raise Company Headquarters on the radio. Within a few minutes the M.T. Corporal arrived with an escort and two flat trucks equipped with winches on their fronts. Byrne was the immediate recipient of as near to a withering 'I told you so' look that a Corporal could give to an Officer without infringing King's Regulations. Gingell was less fortunate and the M.T. Corporal, having heard with increasing incredulity what had happened, in a broad Yorkshire accent cast doubts on Gingell's legitimacy, his competence as a driver and gave a brief review of the unpleasant duties that would be his lot in the weeks to come. The last-mentioned started immediately as Gingell, in his best uniform, was instructed to wade into the sloppy black mud and attach the cables from the winches to the rear of the slowly disappearing Scout Car.

Byrne watched this activity seated under a rubber tree, cradling his carbine and giving an unconvincing impression of being in charge. He had high hopes of the winches. Many times they had been used on jungle tracks. Without fail, when trucks had become bogged down in mud, by wrapping the hook and cable round a tree, the trucks had wound themselves out of trouble. This time it didn't work. A heavy, deeply-embedded Scout Car was just too much. The cables went taut, the wheels of the flat trucks were chocked, the engines revved but the solidly built Scout Car didn't budge. The only crumb of comfort was that, the bottom half of the vehicle having by now disappeared, it stopped sinking. The M.T. Corporal sent back for more vehicles, three more flat trucks arrived. The cables were attached but the combined efforts of all five failed to produce anything more than an almost imperceptible lurch towards dry land. It was now mid-afternoon. Byrne had the Bren guns removed, correctly forecasting that it would be difficult enough explaining the loss of the Scout Car without adding two Bren guns to the total.

The M.T. Corporal reluctantly decided it was necessary to summon outside help and went back to Camp to request a recovery vehicle from the REME Light Aid Detachment based at Battalion Headquarters. He reported to the Company Commander who agreed this was the only available course of action. A recovery vehicle was promised in four hours. In the interests of safety, the Company Commander diverted just-returned 7 Platoon to guard the proceedings. 7 Platoon Commander dispersed his men in a large circle around the area and then sat by Byrne with the intention of extracting the maximum amusement out of Byrne's discomfiture.

It was dark by the time the recovery vehicle arrived. In the glare of headlamps, Byrne was impressed with the speed with which the REME Corporal in charge backed up the imposing and workmanlike vehicle to the edge of the swamp and had cables attached to the Scout Car from the hook of the powerful crane on the back. With the advantage of upward as well as horizontal forces being exerted, the Scout Car was slowly pulled out of the mud, undamaged but filthy and smelling horribly.

Byrne was greatly relieved. Not being fully acquainted with the minutiae of the rules and regulations covering such occurrences, he had not been sure, if the Scout Car had been lost, whether a Board of Inquiry, a Court Martial or a stoppage of pay would be his lot. Or indeed, some combination of all three. The convoy returned to Camp. Byrne to grin sheepishly, listen to the shafts of humour of his fellow-Officers and resign himself to an absence of some pleasant eating and drinking engagements; the equally luckless Gingell to the prospect of many hours thoroughly cleaning the Scout Car, undoubted relegation to driving the water truck, plus cleaning the remainder of the Company's transport and any other tasks of an unpleasant nature that occurred to the M.T. Corporal.

On Monday, as a result of some information received, they had discovered yet another small food dump. Again, the handful of tins was hidden in a large hole cut into the bank of a river. The tins were punctured and left where they were, in the hope that some hungry bandits would eventually visit the site to find the tins of rotting food. On the assumption that where there is a food dump, a bandit camp cannot be far away, 8 Platoon had searched the area for tracks and any signs of a bandit presence. They had found nothing. The following day the Company Commander ordered all three Platoons into the area for a wider and more thorough search. In a prolonged torrential Malayan downpour, they drew another blank.

Wednesday, however, was supposed to be 8 Platoon's day of rest. After breakfast, some enjoyed a morning siesta or wrote home, others found the energy to kick a football about in spite of the oppressive humidity following the rain the previous day; a conscientious few cleaned their weapons in a desultory manner. Byrne sat on the verandah in front of the Mess, read an old copy of the *Yorkshire Post* while calculating whether he could afford the three pounds plus for a very short telephone call the following week to his girlfriend, or whether he should buy a new badminton racquet. Even with the addition to his pay of the Local Overseas Allowance, the size of the monthly draft into the Hongkong and Shanghai Bank left little for extravagances. He made up his mind and walked over to the Signals Tent to ask the Signals Sergeant to book the call.

Thursday had been quiet. 8 Platoon had not been earmarked by the Company Commander for any operations. The C.Q.M.S had stores to be returned to Battalion H.Q. that morning and some ammunition and new tents to pick up. Byrne volunteered the whole Platoon, instead of the customary section, to escort the C.Q.M.S.'s truck. In spite of the moderate exertions earlier in the week, another day in camp, with nothing to do, did not appeal. No-one objected, a ride on the flat trucks and a chance to visit the better-stocked NAAFI in Battalion H.Q. was worth the forty-mile-round trip. Mixing business with pleasure, 8 Platoon practised ambush drills on the outward journey. These consisted of Byrne, in the leading vehicle, firing a shot in the air as they passed along a stretch of road which looked ideal for an ambush. The convoy then came to a screeching halt; the soldiers would jump into the side of the road while the trucks were still in motion. The Platoon then quickly found the most suitable firing positions available, keeping their heads down but looking round for likely places where the bandits might be dug in. They did this five times. After the first three practices the members of the Platoon began to think their leader was perhaps overdoing it somewhat. Brockley and Hird, who had twice found the verges into which they were required to jump and take cover were very muddy, were convinced this was the case.

They arrived just before lunch, Byrne in time for a long gin and tonic and a curry lunch in the civilised surroundings of the H.Q. Officer's Mess; an occasion made even more pleasant on this occasion by the Adjutant, who almost verged on the friendly. 8 Platoon, as ever, equally enjoyed the opportunity over bacon, eggs and beans in the NAAFI of pointing out to the drivers, clerks and storemen the difference between real jungle fighters and idle and cosseted base-wallahs.

For the journey back, Byrne had planned several long detours along minor roads the Platoon had not previously explored. It was on one of these that the Scout Car struck a pig that dashed across the road. It was only a glancing blow but though the pig looked from the outside to be undamaged, it was dead. Within seconds a Chinese appeared and, singling out Byrne as the man in charge, poured forth an agitated mixture of Cantonese and Malay. To Byrne, whose knowledge of Cantonese extended to its equivalents to 'come here' and 'hands up', it meant nothing. Persuading the Chinese to speak Malay, from the odd word he understood, he gathered that he was about to be sued and the damages would be high. While still trying to put together in his head suitable words for the occasion, Sergeant Lennox appeared. In slow but deliberate Malay, with the assistance of the C.Q.M.S. who had more than a passing grasp of the language, he pointed out to an increasingly bemused local inhabitant, the precarious position he was in. His difficulties, according to Sergeant Lennox, were a flagrant breach of Negri Sembilan State Regulations. These, it appeared, required on pain of large fines and possibly imprisonment, that pigs should be kept fenced in and that on no account should they be allowed to stray on the public highway. Furthermore, damage caused by any stray pigs was to be made good by the pig's owner, the gravity of any such offence was, of course, increased if the damage was to a vehicle which was the property of His Majesty the King. Byrne marvelled at Lennox's ingenuity and glanced at the undamaged Scout Car and the very dead pig. In his most sonorous tones, made more forbidding by his Scottish accent, Sergeant Lennox then demanded to know whether the owner of the pig had anything to say that might dissuade his Officer, who was obviously very annoyed and quite rightly was intent on doing his duty, from reporting the obvious crime that had been committed to the authorities. There was no reply from the now dumbfounded Chinese. Sergeant Lennox, seizing the opportunity, said that under the circumstances, his Officer might be persuaded, out of the kindness of his heart and in the interest of good community relations, to give him a few dollars and remove the evidence. The offer was immediately accepted. Byrne produced a handful of dollars and the pig was tied to the back of the Scout Car. Pork was on 8 Platoon's menu that evening.

It was Friday. The telephone rang in the Signals Tent. On the line was the Inspector from the local Police Station. Byrne, the Orderly Officer, was summoned. The Inspector said he had a Malay in his office who insisted he had seen bandits outside his village. Personally, the Inspector thought that the alleged bandits were figments of an overheated imagination. However, he had no men to spare and the nearest Police Jungle Squad was away in the next State. Would C Company care to take a look? The bandits were supposed to have been seen only a mile up a track behind the Police Station itself. Byrne said he would ring him back and huried off to consult the Company Commander. The Company Commander found no difficulty in making a decision. If there were bandits, however unlikely that might be, he wasn't going to have them flaunting themselves in public in his area. If there weren't any bandits, Byrne and ten men from 8 Platoon could do with the exercise and didn't the Commanding Officer insist on co-operation with the Police? He would ring the Inspector himself to tell him Byrne was on his way. A strong section from the Platoon was quickly assembled and within thirty minutes their two trucks drew up outside the Police Station.

Inside, the would-be informer was almost beside himself with frustration and excitement. The Inspector had got the full story. Only a few yards away from the station was a track which led up into the jungle from a small group of Malay dwellings. The Malay, while walking up the track with the intention of collecting firewood, said he had seen, in the middle of a small clearing through which the track ran, three Chinese bandits sitting down, chatting, smoking and playing cards. He had immediately turned and fled. He didn't think the bandits had seen him. He had never seen bandits before near his village. Altogether, he was obviously most upset by the whole affair. If it became rumoured his village was visited by bandits, which was not true, they could be fenced in and restrictions placed on their movements? In short, what were the Police and the Army going to do about it? Further questioning revealed he had not noticed if the alleged bandits had any weapons with them. As he pointed out, he had had no intention of staying to find out. What was certainly revealed was the Malay's hearty dislike of the Chinese and Chinese bandits in particular.

The section of 8 Platoon advanced up the track slowly and warily. Once through the village, the track narrowed rapidly as it ran further into the jungle. Byrne closely followed Brockley and Hird with the Malay acting as guide close behind. Behind came Sergeant Lennox with Lance Corporal Spratt and his Bren gun, then the rest of the section. The Malay understandably became less belligerent and more apprehensive as time passed. He then began to look puzzled and it became obvious to Byrne, as they went through small clearing after small clearing, that they had long passed the spot where the Malay had said he had seen the bandits earlier that afternoon. By this time, Byrne was half-convinced from the

minute-by-minute changes of expression on the face of the Malay, as well
as him keeping an increasingly longer distance behind the leading scouts,
that he had seen something. Unfortunately, whatever he had seen, seemed
to have been long gone.

Byrne was about to give the order to turn about, as he had no intention
of taking part in an unscheduled patrol to the edge of the Company's
boundary when, from a few yards behind, the quiet of the afternoon was
broken by automatic fire; several controlled short bursts from the Bren
gun and two very long bursts from what sounded like Sten guns. Bullets
whined into the trees over the heads of Byrne and the leading scouts who
dropped on to one knee as they swung round to see what was happening.
Fifteen yards behind they saw Lance Corporal Spratt, still standing,
changing the magazine on his gun which he was pointing half-right off the
track. Sergeant Lennox was charging into the trees at great speed in the
direction Spratt's gun was pointing, closely followed by the rest of the
section. The Malay had wisely gone to ground on the other side of the
track. Byrne and the leading scouts could only watch. Within seconds,
Brockley started firing with his Owen gun up the track in the direction
which they had been going. There was a rifle shot and the bullet sizzled
through the air a few inches from Byrne's left ear. He once again felt a
sinking, dead feeling in the pit of his stomach. He and Hird turned.
Brockley had spotted out of the corner of his eye, the three bandits
sprinting across the track from right to left, twenty-five yards away, as if
all the devils in hell were after them. Hird joined in and loosed off a burst
into the patch of jungle into which the bandits had run. Byrne, fear having
quickened his reflexes, was slightly quicker on the draw. He fired one
hastily aimed shot from the shoulder at a flash of khaki shirt disappearing
into the greenery, before suffering the indignity of a jam in his carbine.
Not that the jam made much difference. There were few second chances in
the jungle. Within a split second of the bandits disappearing, Sergeant
Lennox and the rest of the section appeared, hot in pursuit. Byrne signalled to Sergeant Lennox to follow the bandits, though he knew the
chances of catching them, let alone seeing them again, were virtually non-
existent. This proved to be the case when, half-an-hour later, the follow-
up party returned, disappointed and sweating, reporting that the bandits
were nowhere to be found. Five yards or fifty miles away, the bandits
would still have been invisible.

While the search party was away, Burton gave Byrne the handset for
him to radio in a report to Company H.Q. Byrne, Lance Corporal Spratt
and the leading scouts then walked over the area and established what had

happened. Clearly an ambush had not been intended. The bandits had been much more surprised than 8 Platoon. From Spratt they heard that, in front of him and to his right, he had caught a fleeting glimpse of what he had thought was a face peering at him from the jungle, round the base of a tree. The face had very quickly disappeared. Using his initiative, Spratt had immediately flicked the safety lever of his Bren gun forward and fired bursts in that direction. There was testimony to the accuracy of his shooting in the bullet scars low down on both sides of the tree trunk. The bandits had run off parallel to the track. One, or probably two of them, from the number of empty cartridge cases on the ground, had emptied the magazines of their Sten guns as they ran. Fortunately for the Platoon, they had made the mistake, common under such circumstances, of firing far too high. The bandits had then, for some unexplainable reason, doubled across the track where they had first been spotted by Brockley. One of them had fired a single unaimed shot from a rifle down the track as he ran across, which had been too close for comfort. The whole episode had been over in seconds.

There was one splash of fresh blood a few yards behind the tree. One of the bandits had been wounded by Lance Corporal Spratt. However, a .303 bullet tended to knock a man down and as all three bandits were last seen running very fast, it had to be assumed the wound was on the periphery of the bandit and not likely to prove fatal. One mildly cheering note was what the bandits had left behind. No weapons, but a full Sten gun magazine, a dozen .303 bullets, a pack of cards, a khaki cap emblazoned with a red star and several documents. The Platoon was disappointed and later that day they agonised over what other tactics might have resulted in a kill. No-one more so than Byrne. As so often in a fleeting contact, luck played almost as important a part as tactics. Though 8 Platoon were unhappy, their Malay informer was ecstatic. He was delighted with the number of bullets fired at the bandits, positively gloated over the splash of blood and was quite convinced the bandits had been taught a lesson they would not forget and would never come anywhere near his village again. He congratulated the Platoon at length and assured them that a report of their sterling efforts would almost certainly reach the ears of the Sultan. Byrne momentarily toyed with the idea of taking him as a character reference to meet the Company Commander, to offset his inevitable comment that he would have preferred to have seen one or two dead bandits.

The Company's own extensive follow-up operation failed to find any trace of 8 Platoon's bandits. The Platoon kept the red-starred cap and

presented it to Lance Corporal Spratt. The documents were rushed off to
the Intelligence Officer. They were of great interest. They showed many
names and provided information on much of the M.R.L.A. organisation in
three States. This, together with existing intelligence, led to the pinpoint-
ing of some areas where there might be camp sites. The Ghurkhas, following up one of these leads, killed five bandits when they surrounded a
camp.

These successes might have been some consolation for Byrne if he had
had the gift of prophecy. At the time, fishing on Saturday seemed as good
a way as any of forgetting there were three badly-shaken bandits somewhere in the jungle instead of three dead ones.

Chapter 13

A Long Shot

The week-old newspapers arrived from home. Over breakfast there was unusual silence as Byrne and his fellow-Officers leisurely brought themselves up-to-date with news from home. Byrne read a letter in the *Yorkshire Post* from a housewife bemoaning that there was still rationing so many years after the end of W.W.II. He made a mental note to take back with him plenty of chocolate, tinned sweets and butter when he returned to the U.K. According to the *Northern Echo*, Middlesbrough A.F.C. was not doing very well but Middlesbrough R.F.C. was still unbeaten. His own local rugby team had yet to win a match. Little seemed to have changed in the many months since he had left Birkenhead. There were pictures of the Yorkshire Dales covered in several feet of snow. Life was unusually easy, it was pleasantly cool that morning and there were no patrols planned for the next twenty-four hours, Byrne felt a slight twinge of homesickness. He turned to the national papers. One tabloid, more renowned for its peek-a-boo pictures and large sensational head-lines than serious reporting, carried an article on the human situation in Malaya. The headline was to the effect that they were the Forgotten Army. Byrne read the article aloud for the benefit of the others. The Company 2i/c, recalling the large size of incoming Company mailbags, wondered who was doing the forgetting; certainly not wives, sweethearts and parents. The Company Commander was more concerned at outspoken criticism in the article of the civilian British population in Malaya. Many of them, according to the reporter, looked down on the Rank and File and made this obvious but did tolerate the Officers. The breakfasting quintet agreed that nothing was farther from the truth in C Company's area. The Company Commander only hoped the Planters' Clubs weren't subscribers to this particular newspaper.

A major operation had been planned which would last over a week. Several battalions, two Regiments of Royal Artillery and the Royal Air Force were to take part. Three of the Yorkshire Fusiliers' Companies had been earmarked to patrol a long stretch of jungle edge. C Company, based well outside the main area of intended activity, was, in military jargon, left out of battle. The Company had been briefed on what was to happen. No-one was particularly disappointed that they were not to take part. They had all spent too many unproductive days on centrally-organised patrols and ambushes before with little to show for them. The Company Commander, entirely left to his own devices, decided his Company would not remain idle. All Platoons would carry out daily patrols on the fringe of the main area of operations decided upon by the Brigadiers.

C Company's morale was understandably high. With the exception of 8 Platoon, which had earned a reputation for discovering food dumps but had not recently shot any bandits, there had been two recent successes. 7 Platoon had chalked up two kills the previous week. Patrolling in extended order across an open area, with rocks interspersed among patchy but high clumps of grass, the two leading scouts had unexpectedly almost walked into a group of five bandits. They were resting, smoking cigarettes, squatting down in a small circle. Mutual recognition had been immediate. Three bandits had got away, pursued by snap shots from the Platoon. The Owen guns of the leading scouts killed two as they turned to run. Two rifles and two bandits' packs had been recovered.

9 Platoon had enjoyed even greater success two weeks before. A local bandit, Ah Chung, with a price on his head of many dollars, had surrendered to the local Police. He was still carrying his rifle and pack. The bandit was in an undernourished state and complained bitterly that the small amount of rice he was being given to eat each day, plus some banana leaves to stew, were not what he had been led to expect when he had joined the M.R.L.A. two years earlier. He had done nothing but talk incessantly since his surrender. From his eagerly given testimony, it was apparent he believed that many bandits, including some very senior in the hierarchy, were becoming increasingly disillusioned. The promised popular revolution had failed to materialise, less and less support was forthcoming from the general population. Slowly disappearing support meant less food, scantier information on the disposition and movements of the Security Forces and more risks for the bandits themselves. Any feelings of doubt in the cause, he explained, were never expressed, as there were still too many hardline party members who were only too willing to organise their equivalent of a court martial and carry out the inevitable

death sentence personally. It was to be some years before the trickle of surrenders grew to a flood.

What was particularly exciting about this surrendered bandit was that Ah Chung had gone to the Police Station on impulse and that his absence would not be noticed straightaway. He had been entrusted with carrying a message from one District Committee Member to another. Ah Chung had only started his journey twelve hours earlier and was not expected back until some time the following day. His instructions had been to leave the message in a pre-arranged hiding place near a disused tin mine just over the State border. He was prepared and eager to draw a map to show where his own small camp was but he resisted all blandishments to lead 9 Platoon to it, claiming he was too weak. It was frequently the case that a bandit, who up till then had been conscientious member of the Party, had regularly attended interminably long evening lectures on Communism and taken part in the shooting of soldiers, policemen and civilians, would enthusiastically give information which was likely to lead to the violent death of his erstwhile comrades. So the minds of disillusioned communists worked; no doubt also swayed by the generous provisions that would be made for them to start a new life by a grateful Government, once they had outlived their usefulness.

The disused tin mine was identified on the map, together with the whereabouts of the old hut where the message containing comradely greetings was due to be left. The information was radioed to the Ghurkhas who set an ambush. Though they waited patiently for a week, clearly by the time it was intended to collect the message, news of Ah Chung's defection had unfortunately reached the ears of the District Committee Member.

9 Platoon were surprised at the location of the camp as shown on the ex-bandit's sketch. Not only was the camp not very far into the jungle but they must have passed nearby several times on previous patrols, sometimes as close as a few hundred yards. The camp was in the bend of a small river. From his general knowledge of the area, 9 Platoon Commander knew he would have no trouble finding it. The problem would be to approach without being seen or heard. Ah Chung was reassuring. Though there could be any number of bandits from five to ten in residence, the two sentries normally on duty came back into camp before dusk. Thereafter, one bandit would stand guard but he would not move outside the perimeter of the camp.

With only the afternoon left, 9 Platoon, carrying two additional Bren guns, moved quickly. The M.T. Corporal rapidly assembled four trucks and urged by the Platoon Commander, made all possible speed to the

carefully chosen drop-off point, the last-mentioned being a careful com-
promise between nearness to the camp and the maximum distance from
the nearest dwellings. The approach work to the general area of the bandit
camp was accomplished without any difficulty. It was getting dark when
the Platoon got close. They hoped fervently that no bandit had been on an
evening stroll and had already reported their presence. If he had, the birds
would have flown. They came across a narrow track which, according to
the sketch, led into the camp. In the fading light the leading scouts moved
carefully along it, making sure that no snapping of a twig underfoot gave
their presence away. The trees started to thin and thirty yards in front they
saw a gleam of light. They stopped. A Bren gun team was placed in
position with three riflemen. The rest of the Platoon withdrew twenty
yards and with great care moved further round the camp perimeter. They
approached the camp once again, this time through thick scrub. Another
section was placed in position. By this time it was only possible to move
by the light of the moon, which filtered through the treetops. The remaining section moved round until they found the track that ran into the jungle
from the other side of the camp. According to the Ah Chung's sketch, it
was at an angle of sixty degrees to the other. The last Bren gun team with
the remaining members of the Platoon went to ground. The Platoon
Commander crept back round the perimeter to the first Bren Gun he had
positioned. His orders to all three groups had been simple and clear: fire
when he did. The section he was with would follow-up into the camp. The
other two must take great care not to fire on them. All three groups settled
down to the wait with nothing to do but watch the darkened camp and
listen to the night-time chirping of the jungle inhabitants and to the distant
splashes from the river which was out of sight on the other side of the
bandit camp.

From one of the small huts a loud voice could be heard. It sounded like
a harangue. Then all was quiet. The light they had earlier seen gleaming in
the deepening dusk went out. Then there was a flash of light from an
electric torch as the camp guard wandered round the camp. About every
hour he walked round, directing the beam at the huts, the ground and
surrounding trees. It was a mystery to the watching members of 9 Platoon
as to what he thought would achieve. It was obvious the possibility that
their camp could be attacked was far from the thoughts of these bandits. In
the light of the guard's torch they were occasionally able to see part of the
outlines of the three huts they had been told about. Everything the surrendered bandit had said had been accurate so far. 9 Platoon spent a sleepless
night, watching and waiting.

At first light there was a mist which shrouded the outlines of the three huts. It was impossible to see clearly what was happening in the camp, even though the nearest small hut was only thirty yards away. At least one bandit must have been on early cooking duty that morning. The listening Platoon could hear the banging of metal pans as breakfast was prepared. The ambushers quietly sucked boiled sweets and ate chocolate as they waited.

The mist started to thin. Automatically the Platoon checked that their safety catches were off. The outline of the huts and the surrounding trees began to become sharper. A half-clad figure appeared from the nearest hut and seemed to yawn and stretch in the grey and chilly dawn. The banging of pans had stopped. A small fire could now be seen on the side of the camp nearer the river. No doubt water had been put on to boil. It was then 9 Platoon sprang the ambush. The first shot that was fired was not by the Platoon Commander. Given a choice, he would have waited a few more minutes until the light had improved, when most or all of the bandits had been in view and the Platoon had selected their targets and taken careful aim. What had happened was that a bandit had appeared behind their position. It was the guard, with a rifle slung over his shoulder and the torch tucked into his belt. Either the guard was feeling particularly keen that morning, or Ah Chung had forgotten to mention that, at first light, it was the custom for the night guard to stroll through the jungle surrounding the camp to check that all was well before going off-duty. It was simply bad luck that he had started his perambulation unobserved by the Platoon and actually ended up behind them. What had been a successful operation so far could have been a failure with the loss of soldiers' lives. The bandit was walking up the track towards the camp, taking a close interest in the track in front of him. He had presumably noticed the smudged imprints of 9 Platoon's jungle boots from the evening before on the slightly muddy track. Apparently their potentially deadly significance had not yet dawned. He had been spotted, still staring intently at the ground, when only yards away from a prone rifleman at the rear of the position just behind the Platoon Commander. The rifleman had no option but to fire. The bandit fell instantly, shot through the chest.

The effect of the single shot on the bandits was almost instantaneous. There were shouts and screams and what appeared in the half-light to be dozens of bandits ran out of the huts and vanished in the mist. Bren, Sten and rifle fire was poured into the camp, sometimes aimed at running dark shapes and sometimes at where it was hoped the bandits would be. The tracer bullets in the magazines helped the Bren gunners keep their bursts on what they hoped were targets. There was no answering fire from the bandits who were panic-stricken and completely taken by surprise. The Platoon Commander just managed to shout his order to cease fire above the din when it became obvious more shooting would have been a waste of ammunition. The Platoon reloaded and advanced very warily through the camp. The silence contrasted with the cacophony of a few seconds earlier. There were two dead bandits on the ground outside the huts, a man and a woman and one badly wounded male. These, together with the dead guard, made a total of three dead and one captured wounded. The Platoon marvelled that more had not been killed, bearing in mind the hundreds of rounds that had been fired into the camp. Five weapons were recovered. There was the guard's rifle, another clutched in the hand of the dead female bandit and a Sten gun and two more rifles in one of the huts. Bric-a-brac in the huts was testimony to the abrupt departure of their occupants. Six packs of personal belongings, including communist tracts and anti-Government pamphlets, were found in and around huts. Significantly little food could be found, bearing out Ah Chung's complaint of short rations. A can of water was just coming up to the boil. From the makeshift beds, there had been either eight or nine bandits in the camp when they had been disturbed. Blood stains on the bank of the river meant that at least one more bandit had been wounded but not sufficiently badly to have knocked him or her over permanently. However, months later, there was a strong rumour of a bandit who had died of his wounds some weeks after the assault on the bandit camp; no lesser person than the District Committee Member, with hundreds of dollars on his head. The very one who had unwisely entrusted his disloyal junior comrade with the message. This rumour was given some substance in that 9 Platoon's wounded bandit later turned out to be his personal bodyguard.

News of the Platoon's success was radioed to a delighted Signals Sergeant, who lost no time in telling an even more delighted Company Commander. He positively looked forward to the Commanding Officer's next visit when he would be in a congratulatory mood. 9 Platoon's success had moved C Company off the bottom of the Battalion's unofficial 'Bandits Killed' League.

The three dead bandits were tied to poles in order to carry them out of the jungle. The wounded bandit was searched carefully, though from his groans he seemed unlikely to present a threat. However, no-one was prepared to risk him having a heroic streak and producing a hand grenade at an inopportune time. He was unarmed. Field dressings were applied to the bullet wounds in the bandit's shoulder and thigh. A poncho and two poles served as a makeshift stretcher. He was watched carefully as the Platoon made their way to the waiting transport. A captured bandit was a rarity.

C Company counted its blessings. The Company had not suffered a casualty for over ten months. Two of the other Companies had not been so lucky. In all, an Officer and three soldiers, all National Servicemen, had been recently killed in bandit hit and run road ambushes. It was, therefore, not too surprising that there was an air of moderate satisfaction in the Company as it prepared for a succession of daily patrols. No successes were anticipated but at least the week would be a civilised one in that they would be returning each evening to a cold beer and a night in their own beds.

When 8 Platoon set off on the first morning, the noise of the shelling and bombing of the big operation could be heard faintly in the far distance. The other two Platoons had already departed and they had had to wait for the first of the returning trucks; the resources of the M.T. section being unusually overstretched that morning. Their patrol was uneventful, as were those of 7 and 9 Platoons. The Company Commander encouraged them over dinner that evening. Perhaps the local bandits, well aware of the concentration of troops elsewhere, might become careless? C Company's Platoon Commanders were far from convinced.

The next day was a little more fruitful. The Platoon was dropped off before dawn. Crossing a road a mile from a village, they walked into a group of tappers cycling to work. Private Rice remarked on the well-loaded bicycle panniers and the bulky bags on some of the tappers' shoulders. They investigated. Six apprehensive Chinese were found to have tins of rice and fish in abundance. Byrne radioed the Company and within the hour the Police Land-Rovers arrived. The local Inspector was provided with a field day. The six Chinese were taken away for questioning and the Inspector set off, not in a pleasant mood, to question the Special Constables on duty at the gate of the village, whose responsibility it was to search everyone leaving. 8 Platoon went off to the estate to which the tappers had been heading. Some impromptu ambushes were laid and the jungle edge patrolled but they found nothing. The Inspector called in to see the Company Commander that evening. The tappers had denied all knowledge of any bandits. Their transparently lame excuses for having so much food on them varied from it being a present for a cousin they were due to meet at work that day to picking up the wrong bag that morning by accident. They would, of course, be charged and eventually fined for disobeying the law on carrying food but no information on bandits had been forthcoming and nothing more could be proved against them. On one matter the Company Commander and the Inspector were both agreed, there must still be bandits in the area.

On the third day, 7 and 9 Platoons were given the task of patrolling into the jungle, the edges of which Byrne had cursorily explored the previous day. 8 Platoon, which by now had acquired a reputation for having a nose for finding illicit food, were again dropped off early many miles away, with instructions from the Company Commander to try and repeat the performance. There was mounting evidence the local banditry were short of food and making their problem even more acute could only pay dividends in the long run.

The roads were quiet that morning. The few tappers' and wood cutters' lorries the Platoon searched were found to be carrying only the regulation amount of food for personal and immediate consumption. Byrne and the soldiers began to be bored. In the far distance the rumble of the 25-pounders could still be heard from time to time, punctuated by the louder crump of exploding bombs as the RAF devastated patches of jungle. Every now and again they could see aircraft in the clear blue sky as they droned towards the target areas. Occasionally, Typhoons made them duck involuntarily as they roared above their heads, only a few hundred feet above the trees.

Byrne struck off into the jungle to look for tracks. They found them in plenty. Pig tracks, man-made tracks and wider tracks which at one time had been used by lorries hauling trees from out of the jungle. The ground was dry and there were no telltale signs of bandit footprints. Byrne decided to follow a narrow track leading up a steep hill. On reaching the top they found a long-abandoned bandit camp of at least Platoon size, tucked away among the trees on the crest. The camp was large and carefully laid out with a kitchen, sleeping accommodation for over thirty, a small hospital and what appeared to be a headquarters building. A rusting bucket with a large hole in it, the remnants of some bandages and two empty .303 cartridge cases were all that had been left behind by the previous occupants. Still visible were traces of four tracks which led from each corner of the camp to sentry posts just below the crest. From these well-selected vantage points, the Platoon admired the panoramic views they gave in all directions.

Byrne marked the position on his map. Though unused for a long time, it might be worth another visit one day, just in case. To mount an attack on such a well-situated camp would take at least a whole Company. He was secretly relieved it had not been occupied when they had found it.

Given alert sentries, the Platoon would probably have suffered casualties and most, if not all, of the bandits would have easily got away. He wondered why the camp had been evacuated. It was several hundreds of yards down the steep hill to the nearest water; it might have been discovered much earlier and no record kept; perhaps there had been problems in obtaining food. A more likely explanation was that the Ghurkhas had at one time been responsible for that area and life had become too dangerous.

8 Platoon rested on the hill, basking in the heat of the midday sun and admired the view for a long time. From afar, the sound of guns firing and shells exploding could still be heard. In the distance, a solitary Typhoon could just be seen racing in and releasing rockets at some unseen target. Tea having being brewed and cheese sandwiches eaten, the leading scouts led the Platoon down the hill. At the bottom they stopped briefly to refill their water bottles, not forgetting to add the purifying tablets, which may have made the water safer to drink but in the opinion of the soldiers, did nothing to improve its quality. The taste and slight smell of chlorine was a small price to pay, as Sergeant Lennox had often pointed out, from catching something particularly nasty from a decomposing dead animal that might be lying in the water just upstream.

Byrne was aiming to bring the Platoon out near a small village from where he would radio in for transport to pick them up. They plodded on for a few more miles until the trees started to thin out and the strong hot sunlight filtered through the overhead canopy. Mid-afternoon, they reached the edge of a deserted paddyfield. It lay between them and a rubber plantation, beyond which lay the village for which Byrne was aiming. The paddyfield was over 200 yards across. There was no-one in sight on the far bank or in the paddyfield. Almost immediately in front of them was the start of a slightly raised path that led across the shallow still water. About halfway, the narrow strip of dry land widened and by the track was a small hut, used by the rice planters during heavy downpours or to eat their lunch. On the far side, separating the paddyfield from the rubber estate behind, was an irregular strip of trees, bushes and lallang. The guns could still be heard rumbling in the distance.

Byrne decided it was suitable country to give his N.C.O.s a chance to exercise their own talents. It was a plan that appealed, as it would give himself a rest and a chance to recover from an acute pain in the lower stomach resulting from an over-indulgence in jungle juice, a condition that had already necessitated three unscheduled stops during the previous hour. He split the Platoon into three parties. One would remain with him around the hut, where they would observe. Corporal Grice would take six men and explore the far bank to the left. Sergeant Lennox would also take the same number of men and explore to the right. They had to be back in two hours, by which time Company H.Q. should have been contacted and arrangements made for transport to pick them up at some suitable rendezvous.

Byrne's small party settled down to provide covering fire if it proved necessary, as Sergeant Lennox and Corporal Grice led their sections across the mini-causeway. The Sections vanished into the greenery. Byrne and Platoon H.Q. settled in around the hut. Burton slung his aerial over the hut to see if he could raise the Signals Sergeant and the remainder somewhat listlessly watched the jungle and rubber edges. The heat was oppressive. There was the hum of flying insects and once the upper branches of the jungle trees thrashed and swayed as monkeys played. Fifteen minutes passed. Byrne, sitting down and leaning against the wall of the hut in the shadow, felt a little better.

From the right came the sound of four bursts of Sten gun fire, followed by several single rifle shots. Then there was silence. Byrne, stomach cramps forgotten, ordered Lance Corporal Spratt to take charge and with batman Rice at his heels, ran as fast as he could over the path and along the edge of the paddyfield.

Sergeant Lennox had carried out his small patrol with strict adherence to the training pamphlet. Every thirty yards the seven men had knelt down in firing positions. Three had observed the jungle edge across the water and three had stared into the shadows between the rubber trees. Everyone listened. They had repeated the exercise every few minutes. It was Sergeant Lennox himself who saw two bandits. Parting the grass he looked across the paddyfield at the jungle beyond. This part of the padi, as it was called in Malay, had not been in use for many many months. In front of him, instead of carefully divided up smooth stretches of water, there were large pools. Many bushes were scattered here and there on small islands created when the water level fell and nature had been left to her own devices. In some ways the area resembled a cleared bomb site.

Sergeant Lennox watched the jungle edge, inwardly not expecting to see anything. After a few minutes and immediately in front of him two figures walked out from among the trees. A few feet from the trees they stopped, looking around. One was carrying a rifle. The Sergeant could not see if the other had a weapon. The Platoon Sergeant hissed a sharp 'keep down' to the rest of his section. Impressed by the urgency in his voice, they froze. The Sergeant released the grass so it closed in front of him and he flattened himself on the ground. Peering through the stems, his face as low as possible, his first reaction was to marvel at the bandits' apparent lack of concern. Though the guns were still rumbling away intermittently in the far distance, this seemed to have given confidence to the bandits. Perhaps they believed the Army was too busy elsewhere to bother to take normal precautions and the Company Commander's hunch was right.

After a brief pause, looking carefully both ways as if they were about to cross a road, the bandits set off across the padi. They did not even try to cross tactically by coming straight across, so minimising the time they would have to spend in the open. The bandits walked from hummock to hummock, splashing through the shallower pools where they had to and occasionally making small leaps to cross the deeper ones. Incredibly, they were intent on keeping their feet as dry as possible, reminding Sergeant Lennox more of raw recruits hesitating before the muddy part of an assault course than hardened soldiers. To the Sergeant's intense disappointment, instead of coming straight at him as he had hoped they would, the bandits' erratic progress took them on a course which would mean they would reach the section's side of the padi well away to the left. There was no hope of moving the section along the rubber edge to form a welcoming party, there was neither the time nor was the cover thick enough. The two bandits were making fairly rapid progress but this was diagonal and they were taking more interest than they should have done in where they were putting their feet. This meant there was just sufficient time and cover for Sergeant Lennox to motion the two nearest members of the section to crawl up to firing positions three yards on either side of him. He did not need to point out the targets. He tapped his Sten gun and himself, then pointed to the two riflemen so telling them they were to fire when he did. The three soldiers pushed their safety catches forward. They had to wait only for seconds but it seemed much longer as their stomachs chilled and hearts beat faster. Their obvious fear was that the bandits could fire back and kill or wound them. There was also an equally strong fear that, though the impromptu ambush conditions in which they found themselves could have been a lot worse, they might not succeed and the bandits would get away. The two bandits' erratic progress was still to the left and Sergeant Lennox waited until they were forty yards away and had emerged from a clump of thick scrub. To have held their fire longer to get an even better target would have meant the bandits would have been farther away and nearer to the shelter of the rubber trees.

The Sergeant quietly rose on one knee, raised his Sten gun and fired off a magazine at the bandits in four bursts. The two riflemen were only a fraction of a second behind. Both bandits immediately dropped to the ground, out of sight in the grass. Sergeant Lennox and the rest of the section waited, guns at the ready, a slight glow of euphoria beginning to creep over them. They were about to advance when one of the bandits leapt to his feet. He ran off at high speed towards a small promontory covered in bushes that jutted out into the padi to the left. His right arm appeared to be hanging loosely at his side. The bandit jinked to left and right as he ran for his life. The section, though not taken entirely by surprise, failed to bring him down. Rifle shots were aimed at the rapidly fleeing figure but his speed and the occasional bushes that got in the firers' line of sight saved him. He disappeared into the bushes and rubber trees. The section waited, weapons at the ready, in case there was a repeat performance from the remaining bandit. There was no movement. Sergeant Lennox, in the hope that the fleeing bandit had been more badly wounded than appeared to be the case, sent three men to search the area where the bandit had last been seen. It was then that Byrne and Rice, almost breathless, arrived.

Byrne sent everyone except Sergeant Lennox to help in the search for the missing bandit. He and the Sergeant advanced cautiously, weapons cocked, to inspect the first. They were conscious that, even if he was dying or even only wounded, there was always the possibility of a final gesture of defiance. As they moved closer they could see the motionless khaki-clad figure. The bandit was lying on his back, dead. Sergeant Lennox took professional comfort in the three Sten gun bullet holes across his chest. There had been no damage from the .303 rifles but it was quite possible that it was one of the riflemen who had winged the second bandit in the arm or shoulder.

Corporal Grice and his party arrived to offer their help. Byrne sent a runner for the rest of Platoon H.Q. and organised a more thorough and planned search of the area. There was no trace of the probably wounded fugitive. He had, however, left a souvenir. His .303 Rifle, with a magazine containing three rounds, was lying where he had fallen. Of much more interest was the fearsome weapon that had been carried by the dead bandit. Tucked in his belt was a shorn-off .303 Rifle with only four inches of the barrel remaining. The woodwork had rotted or been stripped off and only the metal working parts, which were slightly rusty, were left. The working parts certainly needed a drop of oil. It had the normal magazine attached and resembled a nightmarish horse-pistol. This improvised pistol would have been an impossible weapon to fire with accuracy and showed that the bandits were not only beginning to run out of food but effective weaponry as well.

A search of the body revealed no papers but a fine selection of fountain pens and enough dollars to provide beer for 8 Platoon that evening. This was not the first time that pens had been found on dead bandits and Byrne speculated that, if fountain pens were rewards, this particular communist must have rendered some valuable services in the past. The dead bandit was later identified as a personal bodyguard of a much more important person in the hierarchy. The latter, unfortunately on this occasion, was probably the one who got away. However, the M.R.L.A. were minus one member and there might be less enthusiasm among the rank and file for a volunteer to fill the newly-created vacancy for a bodyguard. None of this, of course, was known at the time and 8 Platoon was only too happy to chalk up a success after so many lean weeks.

The Company Commander, though he would have been more pleased to have been able to report two dead bandits, was able to claim vindication of his tactical theory. He was even more pleased to point out to the Commanding Officer that one of his sections had killed a bandit, which was one more than during the entire major operation. Bombs, shells and saturation patrolling may have disconcerted the bandits but they had lived to fight another day.

Chapter 14

Farewell

Byrne found the weeks before his return home strangely disconcerting. Company H.Q. and 7 and 9 Platoons had been moved to a new location in an adjoining State, leaving 8 Platoon to look after the old Company area for five weeks on its own until Ghurkhas arrived to take over. To his minor frustration and not helped by being a little overwhelmed by the responsibility thrust upon him, Byrne found that guarding the camp and providing escorts for essential truck journeys left very few soldiers for operations. As the Battalion itself was due to sail for home in the not too distant future, for some time departing soldiers had not always been replaced. Slowly decreasing numbers and routine duties that could not be avoided meant that each day only six or seven men could be mustered for a patrol or an ambush.

Though there were daily telephone conversations with Company H.Q., the absence of the rest of the Company began to make Byrne feel increasingly lonely. Living on his own in the Officers' Mess bungalow was eerie. He missed the occasional game of mah-jong and the good-humoured disparaging remarks the Platoon Commanders made about the abilities of each others' commands. More eerie was patrolling with an under-strength Section. Not that both he and Sergeant Lennox hadn't done this before. Byrne wondered why he felt uncomfortable. Slowly he came to realise it was not the responsibility of looking after the old C Company area nor the low numbers he was able to take out on patrol. It was fear. Not so much a physical fear of bandits but a growing concern that one of 8 Platoon or himself might be wounded or even killed by a lucky enemy shot. Having survived for so long, it would have been heartbreaking for 8 Platoon to suffer casualties during his last operations in Malaya.

The bandits refused to give battle and 8 Platoon survived intact. A Company of cheerful Ghurkhas finally arrived and after a brief handover,

128

Byrne and his men climbed aboard their trucks for the journey upcountry to rejoin C Company.

He had only a few days in his new surroundings. Time for a last three-day patrol before handing over the Platoon to Sergeant Lennox. He returned the salute of the sentry at the gate from the Land-Rover that took him and his luggage to the station.

Byrne sat on the patio of the Officers' Mess in Singapore and thought of his 8 Platoon still sweating, getting bitten by mosquitoes, patrolling and ambushing. It was Friday and by then, according to his instructions, he should have been halfway home. The chartered Avro York aircraft had landed on Wednesday and had been due to take off on the return flight on Thursday. Officially he had been told there were technical problems with the aircraft. Unofficially, he was told by the Mess Steward that the aircrew had had a monumental party on Wednesday night. It was not until Saturday that they felt up to starting the return journey.

The last few days before leaving the Battalion had gone quickly. He remembered with nostalgia the beery, very noisy and friendly party 8 Platoon had insisted upon. He had thought of home. The C.Q.M.S. had given him a large box to send by sea. In this he had packed tins of butter, sweets and chocolates, items still rationed at home, for his parents and girlfriend.

Even in the last twenty-four hours he had spent in Battalion H.Q. the Adjutant had kept him busy. He arranged for him to be Orderly Officer and to pay out H.Q. and Support Companies. The order had been accompanied by dire threats as to what would happen if the final balance on the acquittance rolls did not exactly match what he had left over after pay parade. Byrne had taken his time. He had no intention of using any of the few dollars he had accumulated to make up any deficiency. The pay parade had been one of the longest ever and the last understandably disgruntled soldiers had been paid in the gathering dusk with the aid of an oil lamp. To his relief, Byrne found he needed only fifty cents to balance the books.

He knew he would miss 8 Platoon. For the rest of his life it would always be his Platoon. Years later he came to realise more and more that for a year and a half he had been privileged to lead a small platoon of British soldiers. Few of them were career soldiers but conscripts, shipped halfway round the world to endure often extreme discomfort, stress and occasional danger in a war of which, till then, they had been only vaguely aware. That they had quickly acquired jungle skills, had retained an unfailing good humour and become comrades-in-arms came from the pride which they had eventually taken in their Battalion, their Company and above all, their Platoon. Byrne hoped nothing would ever happen to harm the unique *esprit de corps* of the County Regiments.

The flight home took four days with stops for refuelling in Rangoon, Karachi and Cyprus and overnight stays in Calcutta, Bahrein and Malta. Byrne remembered glimpses of temples in Rangoon and leaving his hotel in Calcutta to wander the streets through the night and seeing the unutterable poverty of the people lying on the pavements. The humidity of Singapore was no preparation for the fierce dry heat of Bahrein which took his breath away. He admired the bird's eye view of the white buildings and green palm trees of Israel. There was a shimmering heat which distorted the horizon in Cyprus. A night in hot Malta was followed by arrival at Blackbushe Airport in pouring rain. Then there was a train journey to York Station and his waiting parents and girlfriend.

They pronounced him gaunt and sallow. He was well over a stone lighter than when he had left but he knew he would never be as fit again. Weeks later his seaborne box arrived. The chocolates were mildewed. The tinned butter was rancid. Waterproof wrapping had not stopped his white mess jacket and shiny sharkskin coat becoming stained beyond repair. He consoled himself with the thought that he had commanded 8 Platoon.